EBEN TYNE,
POWDERMONKEY

BY PATRICIA BEATTY

Be Ever Hopeful, Hannalee
Behave Yourself, Bethany Brant
Charley Skedaddle
The Coach That Never Came
Eight Mules from Monterey
Lupita Mañana
Sarah and Me and the Lady from the Sea
Turn Homeward, Hannalee

EBEN TYNE, POWDERMONKEY

PATRICIA BEATTY
AND
PHILLIP ROBBINS

MORROW JUNIOR BOOKS
NEW YORK

Inquiries should be addressed to William Morrow and Company, Inc.,
105 Madison Avenue, New York, NY 10016.

Printed in the United States of America.
1   2   3   4   5   6   7   8   9   10
Library of Congress Cataloging-in-Publication Data

Eben Tyne, powdermonkey / Patricia Beatty and Phillip Robbins.
p.   cm.
Summary: A thirteen-year-old powdermonkey in the Confederate navy
joins the crew of the ironclad Merrimack in a mission to break the
Union blockade of Norfolk harbor.
ISBN 0-688-08884-8
1. United States—History—Civil War, 1861–1865—Naval operations—
Juvenile fiction. 2. Merrimack (Frigate)—Juvenile fiction.
[1. United States—History—Civil War, 1861–1865—Naval operations—
Fiction. 2. Merrimack (Frigate)—Fiction.]
I. Robbins, Phillip. II. Title.
PZ7.B380544Eb   1990   90-35330
[Fic]—dc20   CIP   AC

To
the memory of
our father,
CAPTAIN WALTER M. ROBBINS, USCG,
an old square-rigger deep-water sailor,
and
to
our mother,
JESSIE PAULINE ROBBINS,
a child of the sea

CONTENTS

CHAPTER ONE

BOY OVERBOARD!

Was it a stone bruise, a cut, or an old blister acting up, or was it just the hot September sunshine burning the bottoms of his bare feet? Whatever it was, Eben Tyne was in no mood to ignore its pain. With a thirteen-year-old's agility, he rolled over from where he lay on the Elizabeth River dock, muttered, and sat up. Grabbing his left foot with both hands, he pulled it to his chest, frowning. Good, it was only a splinter from the rough dock planks. Grasping the sliver of wood firmly, he jerked it out.

Beside him, his best friend, Jason Owens, mumbled, "What're you up to, Eben? It's too hot to be moving around. What's wrong with your hoof?"

"A dock splinter, that's all. I got it out. It didn't pain me bad enough to cuss over more than I just did."

"Holy crow, it's hot today," Jason repeated. "It's like breathing water and air mixed up together."

Eben nodded as he ran his fingers through his shaggy, sun-bleached light brown hair. His long face, sprinkled with freckles that marked him on the waterfront of his port town as Captain Tyne's only son, was troubled as his eyes swept Norfolk Bay to the north of the dock. "Maybe we won't be getting a breeze today," he said. "Maybe we can't go out oystering in the *Sarah*."

"Well, the day ain't over yet," Jason reminded him.

Eben looked down at his thin, lanky friend. Although Jason was his own age, he was shooting up to be tall. Red-haired, dark-eyed Jason had always seemed to Eben to be a bunch of parts tied together with string. Where Eben—shorter, more muscular, and chunky—walked, Jason floated over the ground. Jason was the best dancer on the Norfolk wharves. His sailor's hornpipe was so amusing that visitors paid to see it. Eben would call the crowd together to watch, then pick up the coins people threw. If he and Jason had a banjo instead of just a whistled tune to dance to, if Eben could learn to play one, they would make some real money! But Captain Sam Tyne wasn't about to put out good hard cash for a banjo—not right now, anyhow. Money was tight in Norfolk, and for a very good reason.

It was wartime! Ships could not leave Norfolk harbor this autumn of 1861 because the port was blockaded by Yankee men-of-war.

Eben's blue eyes went back to the funnel-shaped bay once more. He said, "I wish we'd fetched a spyglass with us so we could see better. It's hard to see the cussed blockaders way out there without one."

Now Jason rolled over and sat up, too. He also gazed seaward past the pale green shallows to deep blue water. He shaded his eyes with one hand, squinted, then made a growling sound in his throat and spat over the side of the dock. Usually mild-mannered, he exploded. "I get mad every time I even think of them being out there waiting, playing cat to our mouse. Cuss all Yankees! I can see them as black dots 'cause their frigates got black hulls. That's enough looking for me right now. I don't want to see them closer up with a glass, Eben. Cuss old Mister Abe Lincoln's navy for bottling up our ships in our bay!"

Eben grunted. "Aye, Jason, Pa says the Union ships are smartly spaced so their cannon cover every inch of the deep water. They came here to keep our trading ships from getting through Hampton Roads and out into the Atlantic, and they're doing just that." Eben spat twice now, too, and added, "It's ten miles to get out to the sea, but to do that, a Southern ship's got to run past that line of Yankees and risk their cannon fire. It's too danged bad we haven't got any ships of our own to go out and blast them out of the bay. I'd sure like to see that happen. But Pa says the Yankees are tight as a drumhead out there."

Jason nodded. He pointed wordlessly to six masts sticking up out of the water. They marked what was left of two big square-rigged ships that had tried only four days past to take advantage of favorable winds to run the blockade. The Yankees' ship cannon had torn the Confederate merchantmen apart.

Eben, who was inclined to be hot-tempered, said angrily, "I see them!" He shivered. "Pa said eighteen men are dead somewhere under them. . . ." He broke off what he was about to say and looked up to the hazy sky and then at the surface of the bay for signs of a wind rising. He found none.

Eben and Jason were not very talkative. Idle chattering was frowned upon in the Tyne and Owens families, who had been plain, God-fearing, seafaring Virginians from Colonial times onward. What one boy knew, the other knew also. They knew that the war between North and South, which had started just this year, was heating up. It didn't appear to them now that it would be over and done with as fast as most folks had believed and hoped it would. After every land battle, they had gone together after school to read the roster of names posted on the courthouse door. Each list edged in black carried more names of men killed in battle than the one before. They had known some of the men who had fallen for the Confederacy, and they grieved for the loss. Being fair-minded, they had tried to tell one another that families up North were sorrowful and sad, too, when they read the lists of their own dead.

But—and it was a large *but*—Northern ports weren't being blockaded by Confederate men-of-war as Southern ports were. Tons of cotton lay baled in the holds of Southern merchantmen while textile mills in England and France were ready to buy it for their looms. The Confederate government needed the money the cotton would bring to keep the war going, but if the ships couldn't go out, money couldn't come in. That was simple to understand.

Eben said almost to himself, "We can't get out and the Yankees can't come in to get at the ships moored here at the wharves. If they try it, they'll run aground on the shoals, or our gun batteries on shore will sink them."

Jason sighed. "Norfolk Bay's been blocked up tight for four months now. Just look at all them ships waiting to sail."

Eben didn't have to look. He knew what he'd see if he turned his gaze toward the Elizabeth River and Gosport Navy Yard. The yard was a very important place that the Yankees had been forced to desert and leave to the South. Eben had never gone there, though he longed to. Ships lay at their berths just about everywhere near Norfolk. Some were large; others were little coasters. Near Craney Island, directly west of him, eight big clipper ships floated idle, with their sails stowed beneath their decks. Eben knew that if a wind came blowing up a storm strong enough to drive the blockaders aground or into narrow waters, some of the ships in the bay would haul up their sails and risk running past the Yankees.

No storm had come up so far, however. Most September winds were just cat's-paws, never powerful, though little squalls could come up at any time, blow briefly from one quarter, then die down and start up in a different direction.

Jason's voice was mournful. "Eben, I miss watching the big old windjammers go over the Rip Raps of Hampton Roads and cross the mouth of the bay into the ocean. I sure liked it when the sails puffed out full and the ship leaned to a heel, didn't you?"

"Aye, Jason, I don't like watching anything in the world more than watching that. It'd be better, though, to be aboard one of them than just seeing it put to sea. But it'd be best of all to be the captain!" Eben's heart swelled at the very prospect. "Just think about sailing to Shanghai or Liverpool or Calcutta or Hawaii or Rio de Janeiro." He let out a sigh that started in his toes. "Just think about taking your own ship around Cape Horn."

Jason Owens laughed. "I think about that all the time! I even dream about mastering my own ship. My pa says a windjammer can sail faster way down at the bottom of South America than the swiftest horse can run. They got strong winds there. I just wish we had a little bit of it here right now."

"Me, too, Jason. Maybe when we're masters of our own ships, we can get a clipper like the *Zephyr* over there. Ain't she a beauty, though? Wouldn't you like to sail on her? Captain Marcus Walter is a friend of Pa's. He says she's ready right now to whip through the blockade like a hot knife through butter if she gets the winds."

Eben's practiced eye went over the clipper moored nearby, admiring her tautly braced rigging and sleek, coal-black hull with the long white stripe painted on it. She was shipshape ready to sail. Captain Walter would pit his ship, which was built for speed, and his seamanship against the Yankee guns. The Lord willing, the *Zephyr* would make it safely to sea. If not, there would be more masts rising out of the bay like forlorn trees and more dead men buried underwater forever. The South needed its sailors to fight, but it needed its trade to survive.

Next to the *Zephyr* lay a trim little brig, the *Patsy Jean*. Portsmouth-built and shipshape, too, with her white masts and green-painted hull, she'd go out into the bay to dare the Yankees when the *Zephyr* did.

Eben asked listlessly, "Jason, do you want to play mumblety-peg? Got your knife?"

"Don't I always have my barlow knife same as you always do? Naw, I'm gonna lay down some more. It's too hot to do anything right now." Rolling over onto his back, his eyes closed, Jason added, "I'd sure rather be out oystering than doing this."

"Who wouldn't? We're sitting here waiting just like our ships are. It ain't as if we'd be in any danger from the Yankees if we went oystering, so long as we stay in that oyster bed in the middle of the bay. They don't ever come in after little fishing boats like the *Sarah*."

Jason laughed sharply. "She's small-fry, too small for them. Your old ketch is too little to bother with, but all the same I hate knowing they got their spy-glasses on us every minute we're out there on the water."

Suddenly, Jason let out a sneeze. After that, he sniffed and said, "I think I can smell a wind coming up! You know how I can sometimes tell a change is coming." He sat up again. "There now, look at the pennants at the fore-topmast of the *Patsy Jean*." He pointed.

Eben's eyes followed his outstretched finger. Aye, her pennants were fluttering. Eben gazed seaward now, shading his eyes with both hands. There were clouds rising on the horizon at last—small, white, fluffy ones blowing in from the sea. Maybe there would be breeze enough for the *Sarah* to go out. The clouds weren't black or dark gray ones. The ones he saw were fair-weather signs.

He got up, leaned down, and impatiently grabbed hold of Jason to jerk him to his feet. "Come on. I'm ripe to leave. It's time for us to go oystering. It's so sticky hot here, it's getting hard to draw a lungful of air. We can cool off in the bay."

"Sure, Eben," said Jason as he came smoothly to his feet in one fluid motion.

The two boys walked to the end of the dock, where the Tynes' old ketch was neatly tied to a piling some three feet below. Eben and Jason dropped lightly to her deck.

Jason stood by silently as Eben, the *Sarah*'s master, prepared to take her out, unlashing the foresail from its boom, loosening the mainsail, and untying the mooring lines.

As the ketch floated away from the pier, Jason took hold of the halyard and pulled the mainsail up to the mast as Eben hauled up the foresail. The *Sarah* moved slowly and gracefully from the piling out into the bay. Her sails were dusky white against the green of the waters, then turned snowy as she sailed into deeper blue seas. The boys sat silent, each one keeping an eye on the threatening Yankee frigates that they knew had spyglasses trained on them at that very moment.

In twenty minutes' time, the ketch was a mile from the dock and over oyster beds in the middle of the bay. The breeze they had enjoyed died, and the two boys stared at one another in disgust. This meant they might have to row the *Sarah* back. Neither one liked to row when he could sail before the wind. It was a lot of work to row in hot weather.

The *Sarah*'s sails flapped to and fro in the still air as the barely noticeable ground swell moved her hull up and down on the mirrorlike surface of the bay. Diamondlike points of light reflected from the sun brightened her paint-peeled hull. They touched her name for a moment, only to dance away and glisten anew at another point. While the ketch drifted with the current, Eben and Jason were busy. They stood in the shaded shelter of the mainsail and manipulated the sixteen-foot-long handles of their rakelike tongs, opening the tongs on the bottom of the bay. Once the boys felt some oysters in the tongs, they closed them and pulled up the handles until the rakes came over the side of the *Sarah*. There the tongs were opened and the trapped oysters were dropped to join a pile on the scarred deck. They worked in silence, but always with an eye gauging their nearness to the Yankee ships. Gripping the deck planks with their bare feet, they moved in harmony with the boat's bobbing.

Finally, their catch was considered big enough by both, so they stopped work, pulled in the tongs, and lashed them to the sides of the ketch's cabin. Finished, the two boys settled in the shade of the big sail, backs snug against the cabin, feet braced on the side rail.

Eben selected four of the biggest oysters and set about opening them while Jason got out the half-loaf of bread he'd brought from home in a sack. Pulling out his knife, a twin to Eben's, he cut the bread into thick slices. Then, reaching into the sack again, he brought out a large ripe tomato and cut it up, too. They ate the oysters with a tomato slice clamped over them and squeezed between the slices of bread. They licked their fingers, glancing at the sky in search of foul-weather signs. Seeing none, they checked the location of the Yankee blockaders, estimated the slow drift of the ketch away from the enemy ships, and lay back for a short nap in the heat.

While the two boys slept, the weather changed with frightening speed. Quickly, it became muggy with an electric-charged dampness. Clouds lowered swiftly where there had been none before. They rapidly grew tall, forming into a dark gray mass that transformed itself hastily into the anvil form of a giant thunderhead. An eerie brass-colored light bathed the *Sarah* and her sleeping crew.

A single *pop* as the mainsail filled with a gust of wind and then hung limp again when the air became deathly still brought the boys to their feet. One quick look about in the strange light and they leaped to their work. Eben saw Jason take three running steps to reach the lee side of the foresail boom as his friend spotted the churning dirty-gray wall of wind and water rushing to slam into the *Sarah.* There was only time for Jason to untie the foresail so it could flap free in the wind. He was still untying the knot as the full fury of the summer squall hit the little ketch.

The gale-force winds leaned the *Sarah* on her ends. Her lee deck was at once underwater and the tops of her masts not more than ten feet from the surface of the bay. Just a few more degrees of heel and she would go down into the bay like a rock.

While Eben struggled to bring the *Sarah* under control, he looked on in horror as the line of the foresail was torn from Jason's hand when the sail popped like a cannon and threw the boom sideways with terrible force. The boom lifted Jason up from the deck as if he weighed nothing and flung him overboard well away from the moving ketch.

Eben watched his friend sink. From where he stood at the boat's helm, he raked his eyes frantically over the choppy waters. He saw Jason's head break the surface. Good, he thought, Jason wasn't stunned by the force of the boom's blow. Thank God! He might have a chance to survive. Praying, Eben turned to the business of saving his ship. There was nothing he could do right now to save Jason—not the way the *Sarah* was damaged. He cried out in helpless fury. The violence of the winds had blown down the ketch's mainsail and broken the hoops that held it to the mast. The sail trailed overboard in the water, for the time keeping the *Sarah* in place like a huge anchor.

As a seaman, Eben knew he was battling winds of more than a hundred miles an hour. Any mistake he might make would be fatal to his ship and to himself, and would surely mean he could not pick Jason up out of the bay. Jason was a strong swimmer. Right now, Jason had to look out for himself and keep afloat!

Eben fought to bring the *Sarah*'s bow into the wind, but the loose-flying foresail made it impossible to steer the ketch as she went skidding over the white-capped bay. He stood at her wheel, yelling his anger and fright at the winds. He steered as best he could, hoping the boat could ride out the squall. *If he could only hold her.* Facing into the storm, he was hit again and again by stinging hail the size of buckshot. From the heat of an early-fall afternoon, the weather had changed to arctic cold in minutes. In the face of the cold and the hail, Eben gritted his teeth and held fast to the wheel, trying to bring the bow of his ship into the eye of the squall.

Suddenly, with a *snap* like a rifle shot, the mizzensail was blown out by a ferocious gust. Ballooning, it swung the stern of the *Sarah* downwind and pointed her bow at an angle just off the center of the storm. High seas crashed over the sides of the little sailboat. Green water was everywhere. He could not see the *Sarah*'s decks anymore but could feel her dive into the breakers, then rise and challenge the next great wave. The shallow cockpit where Eben stood was full of seawater. It came in so fast that the scuppers could not clear it. It only sloshed out as the *Sarah* gyrated. Along with the water came dozens of sharp-shelled oysters washing along the deck toward his feet. Each time Eben tried to move his feet to get better leverage on the helm, he had to kick oysters away. With each kick, he got a new cut on his bare feet. The pain stung him to tears.

The air was so full of rain, hail, and spume, he couldn't see the *Sarah*'s bow only thirty feet before him. Hanging on grimly, still master of his little ship, Eben endured, sometimes praying, sometimes cursing the sea, and always shouting out Jason's name, hoping his friend could hear him.

Time seemed endless to Eben Tyne, yet it was only fifteen minutes before the white squall passed the *Sarah* and continued up the bay past Hampton Roads. The sun peeked out for a second, then reappeared to shine brilliantly. The bay quickly turned calm except for a slightly choppy sea and a light breeze.

As soon as the storm had passed, Eben tied the wheel and jumped to the top of the cabin. *Jason!*

Where was he? Eben looked everywhere over the water, but there was no sign of him. A groan came deep from Eben's chest. He shinnied up the mainmast to get the best view possible and again looked carefully around. Oh, Lord, there was no Jason! Had his friend drowned, thinking he'd been deserted?

What should he do? Eben knew the *Sarah* had been blown along the path of the squall. She would have moved more than Jason would have treading water. His friend should be just about where he was when he'd been knocked overboard. The *Sarah* would have to sail back and forth over the path of the squall to find him—if he was still alive.

Reciting the Lord's Prayer over and over, Eben captured and tied down the runaway foresail, pulled the soggy mainsail to the deck, and hoisted the mizzensail. Now he set the ketch to crossing and recrossing the track of the storm, sailing and calling out his friend's name over and over in his loudest and deepest voice so it would carry farther over the water. Frantically, he searched for a sign, any sign. Each time he tacked the *Sarah* to bring her to a new course, he became more frightened. Time had to be running out for Jason.

Eben had just finished his fourth tack and was turning the *Sarah* for another run when, from the corner of his eye, he saw a pale glint in the sea that was not reflecting the sunlight. Shading his eyes with both hands, he saw something white—an arm waving! It was waving just above the surface of the water. Jason!

Joyously, Eben brought the *Sarah* to where a spitting and gagging Jason treaded water as he awaited her. With a quick turn of her wheel, Eben moved his ship's rudder to bring her bow directly into the breeze. Her sails flapped and the ketch primly slid to a stop so Eben could give Jason a hand to the deck and then a ferocious hug of welcome.

As soon as he was on board, Jason leaned over the side, rammed his finger back into his throat, and rid himself of the water he'd swallowed. Next, he felt the pocket of his overalls to make sure his precious knife was still there. It was. Jason was just fine now, his old self.

He said thickly and with no word of thanks to Eben, who needed none, "I'm lucky I didn't get stung by sea nettles. It wasn't smart of me to get on the lee side of that boom."

"It sure wasn't," agreed Eben with a shake of his head. "Don't you do that again." He was too relieved even to speak angrily.

Jason moved to the mainmast and began to repair the mainsail mast hoops. Eben gazed at him carefully, and, seeing he was all right, looked away and began gathering the oysters into a basket.

Soon the mainsail was set and the *Sarah* was on her way back to port as if nothing at all had happened.

Eben and Jason both knew that a squall was something that could come along at any time.

While they sailed for home, they kept a close watch on the water alongside the ship's hull. The squall's passage would excite the blue crabs and make them come up to swim on the surface. The boys went back to work swiftly. Dropping the mainsail to slow the ketch, Jason steered as Eben stood at the bow with a dip net tied to the end of one of the oyster tongs. Yes, the crabs were there, some big ones among them. In less than five minutes, Eben had a two-gallon wicker basket nearly full of delicious crabs.

There was just enough time to lash the oyster tongs again to the sides of the cabin before the *Sarah* nuzzled up to the old dock. Once her sails were dropped and she was tied up to the piling, Jason put the baskets of crabs and oysters onto the dock as Eben set to work to furl her sails and lash them to her booms. Next, the *Sarah*'s decks were washed down with buckets of water. Finally, the two boys, baskets in hand, started down the dock toward the shack at its end. The old man who generally bought their catch lived there.

Not a word was said about the squall as they walked, neither of them realizing that that summer storm would change Eben's life for years to come.

· CHAPTER TWO ·

STRANGE NEWS AND A STRANGER REQUEST

The old man had watched the two boys walk toward his shack and now came out to greet them. Speaking in the strange-sounding dialect of his boyhood home in England, he asked them, "Wot ye lads be havin' for me today? I be takin' it wotever it be, I think." Gnomish, he scuttled sidewise as a blue crab would and peered into the catch baskets. "Crabs, eh?" His eyes got wider as he gauged the good size of them. They would bring high prices when he sold them from a barrow in Norfolk.

"Aye, they can be yours if your price is fair," said Eben.

"It will be. I'll give ye five cents for all this fine catch in the two baskets.

"Nay," piped Jason, who enjoyed driving bargains. "We want a whole ten cents."

"Ye be hard on an old man, lads. Seven coppers then for all."

"So be it," answered Eben, nodding to Jason that they should set down the baskets at the door of the fish shack. They could come back later for them and stow them aboard the *Sarah.*

After counting out the coppers, one by one, into Eben's palm, the old peddler turned to conversation. As he pointed a leathery arm toward the bay, he said, "That squall . . . she be a fierce one, eh?"

Eben's eyes were arrested, as they always were, by the sight of a blue butterfly tattooed on the back of the man's hand. For certain, this old one had not been a peddler all his life. He'd been a deep-water sailor. That butterfly tattoo meant he'd been to Shanghai in faraway China. Eben always searched for tattoos on any sailor he met. They told stories to him, a captain's son.

Eben answered the old man's question. "Aye, sir, it was a brisk squall. Fare you well now." Had he seen a look of admiration come into the man's eyes? This old sailor would know it had been touch and go for them on Norfolk Bay.

He and Jason walked into Norfolk richer by seven

cents, but the amount presented a problem to the boys. Eben finally figured out what he should do to be absolutely fair. He counted out three of them into Jason's hand, and then he walked to a large flat rock beside the nearest whitewashed picket fence, lifted the rock, and slipped the extra cent underneath. Jason laughed. They continued along the street, headed for home, while Jason's wet clothing dried out in the heat.

Four young Confederate soldiers came walking toward them. The leader was not more than nineteen, only slightly older than the other three. All were dressed in gray wool uniforms with yellow piping on the cuffs and trouser legs. Eben could tell that they were cavalrymen by the crossed sabers on their hats. The oldest one had been wounded. He carried his arm in a sling, while the neatly patched hole in the sleeve of his jacket showed where a bullet had hit his arm.

The tall blond cavalryman spoke to both of them. "You're brave lads. We seen you out in the storm just now. A man on the pier gave us a look from his spyglass for a little bit. We passed it around. I tell you, I'd rather be where I got this"—he pointed to the patch on his sleeve—"than be out where you was. Take care of yourselves now. Don't you go drown. The South can use folks like you later on when you grow up some more."

Eben answered, "That's kindly of you to say that.

We did our best, Jason and me. I hope we'll serve the South the way you did. If the war goes on long enough, maybe we can. Where'd you fight?"

"Just west of here. We come up against a Yankee regiment that had got by Richmond's forces. Our old General Macgruder gave the job of licking the Yankees to us, the First Virginia, and we done it. We come here only for the day to fetch back Tom here's brother." He pointed to a pale, plump soldier behind him. "Harry got killed in the battle. Tom and Harry wanted to be fetched back home if they fell. We fetched Harry." Having said his piece, the soldier nodded and moved on. The others went with him.

Eben looked to Jason and saw that his face was as coldly somber as his own. What was happening in Virginia during the war was no secret to them. The war was something they lived with every day. Although they were seafaring folks, they knew of the land war as well as of the blockading. They knew that only five months past, the Confederates had captured Harpers Ferry, also in Virginia, and held it for nearly two months as they took away guns and machinery the South needed for her war effort. Just four months ago, the bluebelly Yankees had pushed the Confederates back nearly to Richmond. At Laurel Hill in the Shenandoah Valley, the South had lost many men in a battle, but in July the Yankees had met their match at Manassas, which they called Bull Run. There, along with more than fifteen hundred dead or wounded, they had lost many cannon and many stacks of rifles and ammunition. Already there had been big battles. Everyone thought there would be bigger ones yet to come.

Eben heard Jason's question: "What do you think of our chances of winning the war? Pa says Southern men are brave and well led."

"That we are, Jason. I reckon we'll win if it's fighting man-to-man. We're tougher than whit leather and better at that than Yankee clerks and pen pushers. Pa says our big trouble will be getting the stuff we need to fight. Up North, they got the mills for making machinery and iron. They got more folks to fight, and they got more ships than we have. We've got cotton, and that's like gold, but we got to get it by the Yankee blockaders to sell it. You know those two foreign ships in the harbor, the English and the French ones just off the point? Pa says they're sitting there at anchor watching to see how good us Southerners do. If we show up strongest, they'll back us up with guns, men, and money. We got to prove ourselves to the foreigners, 'cause they're like a hungry sea gull ready to go where the pickings are best. We just gotta bust our way through that line of Yankee frigates one way or another . . . and soon."

"Aye, Eben, you're right. We got to."

As they talked, they marched homeward, knowing

from habit that dinner was ready. As Eben went inside, he was promptly escorted out by his little, fair-haired mother, with a bar of soap in his hand and a clean towel. Sloshing water from the pump into the tin washbasin, he looked across the pastureland the Tyne and Owens families shared in common and saw Jason doing the very same thing. Eben grinned.

Hardworking, simple people who made their living from the sea, the Tynes and Owens were not slave owners. Neither family approved of the idea of black slavery, though as loyal Virginians they supported the cause of the South and states' rights over the rights of the union of states. They did their own labor on their land, ships, and in their houses. The work was often dirty and hard, but they did it themselves.

Once he had washed to his mother's satisfaction, Eben went inside the large kitchen, which held a huge cast-iron stove where all the cooking and baking were done. He was always powerfully concerned with food and looked appreciatively at the platters. There was chicken with fluffy dumplings on the table. Ears of steaming corn rested beside a bowl of baked green squash. A cut-glass jar of his mother's wonderful strawberry preserves poked its most welcome head up alongside the loaf of hot bread.

Now Amanda Tyne nodded at her son to sit down as Captain Tyne held out her chair for her. Then he went to sit at the opposite end of the table. Eben slid into his place between them and listened while his dark-bearded father said grace. As usual, he prayed too long for Eben.

In Captain Sam Tyne's house, dinner was eaten slowly and in silence, so Eben concentrated on the overflowing plate in front of him.

When everyone was finished, his mother hastily cleared the table and set out fresh milk and an uncut blueberry pie. She put the teakettle on the stove again, usually a sign that someone was expected. But who? Eben didn't ask. He would find out soon enough.

At loose ends, he picked up the block of pine he was whittling into a mallard duck decoy, opened his barlow knife, and began to carve, deftly shaving the wood to the floor. He would use that later on in the kindling box.

The sharp blade had just dug out the last little nick of wood to make the duck's bill when there came a knock at the door. Yes, sir, it was company! Eben caught his mother's commanding eye. He set his decoy aside and answered the door. It was the Owenses, all of them—Mr. and Mrs. Owens, Jason, and Becky, his sister. Becky, an imp of a redheaded girl, offered a plate of peanut cookies to Eben. He invited his neighbors inside and then carried the cookies to the table. Soon the two families were eating pie and cookies and talking back and forth. Something had brought them together tonight, Eben thought. *Something was up!* He wondered whether it had anything to do with what had happened that afternoon aboard the *Sarah*. He hoped not. Maybe he and Jason would be forbidden to sail her anymore. That wouldn't be fair, though. The squall hadn't been their fault.

Captain Tyne was a ship's captain, a master mariner. So was Captain Owens, but he carried the papers of a chief steam engineer, too. Both men hired out on merchant ships sailing out of Norfolk, but neither sailed anymore, thanks to the Yankees' blockade.

Joseph Owens said to Eben's father, "You do the talking, Sam."

"Aye, that I will. What I have to say, children, is already known to your mothers." Sam Tyne's voice was low and solemn. "What I'm going to tell you has to be kept a secret. It must not reach the ears of the Yankees. Within the week, Captain Owens and I will be gone from here. Virginia has called both of us to duty. There's a ship waiting for us now. We'll sail on her to Le Havre, France, where we'll be working for the cause of the Confederacy, buying machinery and weapons. We don't expect any trouble running the Yankee blockade, as we're to sail from another Southern port. We'll cross the sandbars there at flood tide. Where we leave from or when, I cannot say. We'll be gone for some months . . . until our business in France is done." He smiled at the three children and added, "We'll bring back a valuable cargo for the South, as well as presents from France for each of you."

While Captain Tyne talked, Eben and Jason glanced

swiftly at each other. The secret port had to be Wilmington, North Carolina. They were sure of that. The ports of Savannah and Charleston were bottled up by the Federals, too, just like Norfolk. Never mind, though, their fathers' secret would be safe with them. Trying to look as if they didn't know the name of the secret port, they turned to look politely at Eben's father as he went on to tell them that each now had the responsibility of the man of the house in his family.

Man of the house, thought Eben with pride. That meant more chores for him, but it also opened the door to new things. He and Jason could now row across the river to the Gosport Navy Yard, a place they had never visited. When they had asked before, they had been told no.

Eben knew that there had been exciting happenings at the yard ever since the night last April when the cowardly Yankees had skedaddled from there and left everything behind as they ran for safety from the attacking Confederate forces. While Eben hadn't set eyes on any of it, he'd been told that there were barrels and barrels of gunpowder there, big cannons, all kinds of rifles, one of the most complete metal forges in Virginia, and tall stacks of cannonballs. There were buildings full of rope, sails, chains for anchors, and construction materials for the dry dock where big ships could go for repairs and outfitting. Now the

South owned all these valuable things of war because the Yankees had run away.

As his father answered a question from Mrs. Owens about the voyage to Europe, assuring her they would all come through all right, Eben thought about the rumor he had been hearing in Norfolk. Secret work was going on right now at the yard. A *special* ship was being rebuilt! Which one it was or what its service was to be, he did not know. However, he would love to find out!

His father's voice interrupted his thoughts. "Eben, while I'm away, be sure to keep the *Sarah* well up in the shoal water by the mouth of the river. One day soon, the Yankees will sail closer in, policing the bay. Anyone close to their line of frigates could get pulled in. Sail a clean course away from them. Be careful, son."

"I will, Pa."

Now Captain Tyne gave him an order. "Eben, there's one thing more. You be on board the *Zephyr* midafternoon Monday. I have need of you then. Come as soon as you've done any homework your teacher gives you."

Eben stared at his father in surprise. What did he have in mind? The *Zephyr,* the fine clipper? He would get to board the *Zephyr?* That would be a treat, indeed. "Aye, Father, I'll be there." Eben glanced at Jason, wondering whether he was to be invited aboard her, too. Visiting her was one of Jason's hopeful dreams, also.

Captain Owens's words stopped that. "Jason, you'll be working with me in the house. There are matters to be put in order before I leave."

Eben could see Jason wasn't happy about working at his home when his best friend would be doing something exciting, but he knew Jason wouldn't complain.

Eben asked his father, "Pa, why am I wanted on the clipper?"

Captain Tyne didn't smile. "You'll find out when you get there and not before."

That night, Eben went to bed with a new sense of importance. He was part of a secret. But what was it? As he lay in bed looking at the ceiling, he thought of that, and of his father's departure, too. Pa would be all right on this voyage. He could take care of himself wherever he sailed. Sam Tyne had often been away from home, and Captain Owens, too. Seafaring men of Norfolk were often away on voyages that lasted for months. The last time Captain Tyne had been away, he had been gone more than a year. Eben had been younger then and had been considered a child. But not now—not in wartime. And his father had said he *needed* him—needed him aboard the wondrous *Zephyr*! Sam Tyne had never used the word *needed* before. He wasn't the sort of man to need anything.

He "manned his own vessel alone," as the saying went.

All through church services the next day, Eben's mind kept wandering from the sermon on giving one's life to the service of the Lord. Once, when the minister spoke about governing flaring tempers, Eben's mother nudged him with her elbow. He knew what she meant, but he wasn't interested in that. So he had a fiery temper at times! He couldn't help it. Besides, all he could think of was the clipper ship. What did Captain Walter want with him? Eben looked at his father, trying to get a hint of it from his face. Sam Tyne looked straight ahead as always, keeping his eye on the preacher. There wasn't anything at all in his face that told his son what he was thinking about, and it wouldn't do one particle of good to ask him, either.

Monday came in with the promise of being a fine day. The sun's early rays caught Eben and Jason in mid-pasture, walking home from the barn their families shared. Each boy carried a pail of frothy milk. Their first chore of the day was now over. Neither one spoke of their fathers' sailing, or of Eben's impending visit to the *Zephyr*.

Once he reached his own back door, Eben did his second chore of the day. He poured milk into the saucer set beside the steps. His mother's big orange cat, Napoleon Bonaparte, approached, taking stately strides toward his dish. Eben patted the crouching animal and went in, putting the pail of milk on the kitchen counter. Washed up and ready to eat, he joined his parents for bacon, steaming hot buttermilk biscuits, lots of rich, creamy gravy, and milk fresh from the cow. He could have had China tea like his mother and father, but milk, he knew, put muscles on a boy. Tea didn't.

While Eben ate, he propped up his battered copy of *McGuffey's Reader* in front of his plate. While he chewed, he reviewed the reading lesson for the day. He had to do well in school today. He couldn't let his teacher keep him there afterward because he didn't know his lessons. He had to go to the *Zephyr*! He was needed there.

Using the last bite of biscuit as a mop, he scoured his plate till it shone, then asked to be excused from the table. Wearing freshly laundered overalls with no smell of oysters and crabs about them, Eben tossed the leather-strap-bound books over one shoulder and went out the front door. Jason and Becky were waiting for him in the meadow, and the three set off for the clapboard school that served their part of Norfolk. After a half-mile walk, they were at the school grounds—and early. The boys set down their books by the split-rail fence, pulled out a much-used old shingle from under it, opened their knives, and began playing mumblety-peg while Becky joined other girls jumping rope. Eben and Jason flicked their cherished barlows up into the air, watching them spin in the sun and sink point-first into the shingle. Counting three for each good toss, taking a point away for each time the knife didn't stick, they were both at the same score of fifteen when their teacher, Miss Mitchell, rang the school bell.

The school day started with penmanship. Eben and Jason used new steel pen points, while some others had to carve sea-gull quills to make old-style ones. By now, the two boys were old enough to write on real paper. Eben didn't like that as well as the blackboard he could erase. Make a mistake in black ink, and you had to stay after school and rewrite the work till you got it right. Not today! He had no time for mistakes and made sure he didn't make any.

He didn't make any errors in reading aloud, either. Next came geography. He opened his book not to Africa, which they were supposed to study, but to his own state, Virginia. He thought of the war as he looked at the familiar names—Newport News, Hampton Roads, Norfolk, and Chesapeake Bay. He saw these places in a new light now. How could the Yankee blockade be broken? How could a Confederate ship slip by? Deep in thought, Eben ran his finger over the map, thinking of the waters he knew so well—their depths, their shoals, their islands. Big ships could not sail in shallow water, but they could control it with their cannons. Did the blockaders have something to do with Captain Walter's asking him aboard the *Zephyr*? *Him!* It was odd. He wasn't four-teen years old yet and wouldn't be for half a year. How could *he* be wanted?

Grateful that he had had to answer only one easy question about the Nile River in Egypt, Eben emptied his mind of the clipper ship he so admired when his teacher began their arithmetic lesson. It was his favorite subject. It was fun adding, subtracting, mul-tiplying, and dividing sums. He would need mathe-matics when he went to sea. A small mistake in numbers could show any ship's location hundreds of sea miles from where she really was. And mistakes in navigation could wreck a vessel and cost many lives. Pencil and paper were all right for a storekeeper, but not for a captain at sea. Sometimes he had to do figuring in his head, and it had to be right.

The last subject of the day was debating. Today's topic was "When a tree falls and no one hears it, is there noise?" One pupil had to speak for it, the other against it. Eben drew the school bully, Jamie Sloat, as his opponent. Short, tough, red-faced Jamie lumbered to his feet and spoke against the likelihood of a noise, but he spoke in a halting voice, gathering his thoughts with trouble. It seemed to Eben that Jamie would rather talk with his fists. In his turn, Eben spoke slowly and clearly, piling fact upon fact as he saw them.

The more Eben said, the more Jamie glowered, knowing who would win the debate and get the good grade. When Eben won, he reckoned Jamie plotted his vengeance, and it would come soon. Jamie wasn't one to wait. Eben sighed inwardly. Jamie held grudges. He always wanted to get even when he felt he had had his toes stepped on.

Eben sighed aloud. He didn't have time to fight today—not when he was expected at the *Zephyr*.

By noon, school was dismissed except for those who had to stay after till three o'clock. Most of Miss Mitchell's pupils started for home. Jamie Sloat had been the first one out the door, Eben had noted. He knew what that meant. So did Jason and Becky. As Eben and the Owenses passed a two-horse wagon hitched near the schoolhouse, Jamie jumped out from behind it and stood before them. Just the sight of Eben made his face turn a darker red. He clenched and released his big whitish fists, then clenched them once more. He was going to challenge Eben Tyne and whip the tar out of him.

"You think you're big and important, but you ain't!" taunted Jamie. "You got bat ears, Eben Tyne. You ain't nothing to look at on the hoof. Your nose runs. You think you're better'n me, and I don't like your dirty face full of freckles."

Eben kept silent, though he had started to boil with anger—both at the insults and at the delay Jamie was causing him.

Jamie crowed, "You're a yellowbelly, too. I'm going to change your face. See!" He put up his fists.

"Go away, Jamie!" piped up Becky while Eben readied himself mentally for the inevitable fray. "You're a half year older than Eben and you're bigger. Pick on somebody your own age and your own size. I bet you'd be scared to do that, though."

This was too much for Jamie. He spun toward the girl and made the mistake of grabbing at her to shake her. Eben leaped forward in fury. The next thing Jamie knew, he was flat on the cobblestones, gasping for breath. Jason had quickly stooped down behind him at Eben's sudden nod, and then Eben had thrown his shoulder as hard as he could right into Jamie's mid-section, knocking him off his feet.

A furious Eben didn't wait for Jamie to scramble up. Enraged, he reached down and jerked him up by his overall straps. If Jamie Sloat wanted a fight, he'd give him one; he'd pestle him! Drawing back his right arm, Eben sent his fist upward into Jamie's face, hitting him on the nose. Blood gushed freely down the front of the bully's shirt and overalls. Filled with the desire to fight, Eben dimly heard Becky's screeching as he hit Jamie in the stomach, making the older boy bend over. Then he saw Jamie sink to the stones and thrash about, holding his abdomen.

Jason sprang forward swiftly and pinioned the heavy-breathing Eben, who was poised, his foot pulled back to kick Jamie.

"No, Eben, that's enough!"

"Don't, Eben!" shrieked Becky.

Eben drew in a deep breath, gasping for control, then shook himself all over like a dog coming out of water.

As Eben withdrew his foot, Jamie snarled, "I'll git you, Eben, and you, too, Jason."

"No, you won't get anybody, you hear! And you leave Becky alone, too," growled Eben, staring down into Jamie's hatred-filled eyes.

Leaving Jamie sitting on the cobbles, the three of them continued walking toward home. Jason warned, "Eben, you better watch out for Jamie. He's a mean one."

Becky said, "I bet Eben would whip him any day and twice on Sundays."

Eben, who was partial to red hair and who thought twelve-year-old Becky mighty handsome, blushed and said nothing.

As they parted in the meadow, Jason asked Eben, "Will you tell me later on what you did on the *Zephyr?*"

"If I can, you know I will. Pa's being awful secret about it, though."

In an hour, Eben's homework was done and the ever-demanding kitchen stove had been fed and its box filled with chopped-up wood.

His mother surprised him by saying that his father,

who was already at the *Zephyr,* wanted him to wear old clothing when he went to the clipper. Her voice had sounded strange as she told him, but in his excitement at going, Eben paid it little heed. He changed quickly and was out the door in no time.

When he neared the clipper, a voice hailed him by name. "Eben Tyne!" A small skiff shoved off from the side of the *Zephyr* to pick him up and take him aboard. I must really be wanted, Eben thought, to be waited for and rowed to her. This had never happened to any other Norfolk boy he knew. None had ever set foot on the deck of the clipper ship, though they all longed to.

As the skiff came alongside the *Zephyr*'s hull, Eben took hold of the rope ladder and climbed on board. He was met by his father, who had stepped away from a small group of men working on something on the deck.

Eben held on to the rope shrouds leading to the mainmast as Captain Tyne walked toward him. As he climbed over the railing, Eben stared in wonder at the huge mast and its thick base, which was nearly three feet across where it passed through the teakwood deck. Gazing straight up, his eyes followed the line of the mast, higher and higher as he counted the five big spars that would hold her sails when she was under way. The masts seemed to touch the sky. To him, the clipper was a thing of great beauty, where power and grace worked together. It would be a pity to see such wonder pass away to steam-powered ships that spouted ugly smoke and stank of engine grease, but it would pass, he knew. Winds could not be relied on. Engine could.

Dropping lightly to the deck, Eben followed his father back to the group of men. Eben recognized Captain Marcus Walter as the big, grizzled, walrus-mustached man who was directing the work. As the boy watched the men, trying to figure out what they were doing, Captain Tyne said, "It's all right, Eben. They know what they're up to. Just watch what we do. Everything will be explained to you in a few minutes. For now, just you watch."

Eben saw nearly two dozen fireclay pots in front of him. Each was about a gallon-size, with holes bored into its sides. What looked like long fingers of lead came out of the holes. These fingers were held to the clay of the pots by sticky waterproof pitch. As Eben looked on in curiosity, a sailor moved from one clay pot to the next, filling each to the brim with black powder from an open barrel set well off to the side. Eben thought he knew what it was—gunpowder. Just as soon as a pot was filled with powder, another man tamped down the black stuff with a blunt stick to pack it tightly in the container. Then a third man placed snugly fitting wooden corks in the open tops of the pots. The last man cemented the corks with pitch to waterproof them.

What were these contraptions? For sure they would

never fit into any kind of gun Eben had ever seen or heard about.

His father finally explained. "These are torpedoes. The lead horns you see are full of sulfur and phosphorus. Break or bend one of the horns, and the two chemicals will start a fire, making the torpedo explode. They'll be anchored just under the water level and will float there." Captain Tyne added, "And they will blow up when a ship's hull hits them. We wanted you here, Eben, because a young person is needed. These men"—he motioned to the sailors who had made the torpedoes—"chose you because they saw how you handled the *Sarah* in the squall." He smiled. "It seems you impressed them. I wish I'd seen you in our ketch the way others did. You had quite a number of interested onlookers holding their breath. Captain Walter had kept his eye on you with his spyglass and asked for the boy who fought the storm in a ketch! He didn't know that you were my son, you've grown up so."

Eben had no words. His father's face bore a look of pride. And it was pride over an accomplishment of his! Holy crow!

• CHAPTER THREE •

A BRUSH WITH THE YANKEES

Wild excitement flooded through Eben. They wanted him because he was a good sailor and they thought him brave, when, to his way of thinking, all he'd done were the things he thought necessary to save his ship and shipmate in the squall. He asked, "What do they need me for?"

Captain Walter came over to him to reply. "So you're young Tyne, eh? Haven't seen you since you were a small lad. Aye, we need you. There's a new moon tonight, so we can expect darkness. We plan to row out in that steam launch over there and set torpedoes in the bay." He pointed to the little side-wheeler *Lucy,* moored near where the skiff had gone to get Eben. "You'll be part of the *Lucy*'s crew." The Captain paused, waiting to see Eben's reaction. Seeing no fear, only eagerness, he went on with a nod. "The *Lucy* will keep to the shallows at first to stay clear of the blockaders, but when she gets out in the middle of the bay, she'll go into the main channel and set the torpedoes there, where the Yankee frigates are sure to be hit. Only four men are going out tonight. They all volunteered. Your father is one; Mr. Wharton, my first mate, is another; and the ship's carpenter, Hiram Stanley, is the third. You'll be the fourth, if you agree. In case of trouble, your young voice will be of great importance to all of us. I watched you the other day, so I know you can do a man's work and not lose your head. Nobody's pushing you to say you'll go, lad. Take some time to think about it."

Knowing that this would be the most important decision he had ever made, Eben looked from face to face of the men around him. In each one, he saw belief in him. He didn't look at his father—he didn't want it to seem as if he was asking for his advice. He had to act his own man here. He said calmly, "Aye, Captain Walter. I be your number-four man."

"Good, lad. Be on board the *Lucy* one hour after dark tonight. She'll be ready."

"Aye, aye, Sir."

"Know ye, young Tyne," warned the old captain,

reverting to the English speech of his youth, "there be danger here for all of ye."

"Aye, Sir, I suspect so," answered the boy, and in sailorlike fashion, he repeated the order, " 'Be on board the *Lucy* one hour after dark tonight.' "

"So be it. Mr. Wharton, go with Eben and tell him what he needs to know."

"Aye, Sir. Let's be with it now, boy," said the first mate, a thick-bodied, auburn-haired man with a pock-marked face.

Once they were in the skiff again and heading back to the dock, Eben pointed to the *Lucy* and asked the *Zephyr*'s mate, "Isn't she sort of big to row? Will we be going out on the ebb tide?"

"Aye, Eben, that we will so the tide will carry us along like a floating log. And our oars will be muffled by rags in the oarlocks so we'll be quiet."

"But won't the *Lucy*'s paddle wheels slow us down when we row, just like a trailing anchor does?"

"I see you know something of paddle-wheelers as well as ketches. True, the *Lucy* will be harder to row because of her wheels. But we'll have a fire in her boiler and have the steam up just in case we have to run for it. Good dry oak's aboard, so when we stoke the firebox, there won't be any sparks or smoke to give us away to the Yankees. Nobody'll know we're even out there till I pull the throttle on the engine.

Then we'll scoot away just like the Yankees did when they left Gosport Navy Yard."

Eben had two more questions: How did his voice fit in? And why were there only four men to the crew instead of the usual nine?

Wharton answered the last question first, reminding Eben it was good seamanship to use only as many men as was necessary, leaving unsaid that it would be better to lose four men than nine. He added that Eben's father and himself, both senior officers, were going because they were best qualified and would set an example for other men who might soon be asked to volunteer for other dangerous duty. Captain Walter would stay aboard the *Zephyr* and would run the blockade at dawn if their night's work was successful and a fair wind held.

Finally, Wharton answered the boy's other question. If they were challenged by the Yankees, only Eben's youthful voice would reply. He would identify the *Lucy* as a fishing boat. And since boys sometimes went out fishing in the dark of the moon, the Yankees would believe him. Even if Eben wasn't believed, the *Lucy* would gain time to start her paddle wheels and escape back to the safe shallows.

Lost in the prospect of the exciting night before him, Eben walked home from the dock without noticing any happenings along his way through Norfolk. He had a thrilling secret, one he knew he could not share with Jason. He muttered to himself, "It ain't much fun to have a secret less'n you can tell it to a friend." Kicking a pebble in front of him, he watched it skip along the cobblestones. This action seemed to help him control his excitement and the rising awareness of the perils he and his father might encounter that night.

Dinner was a particularly fine one. As Eben tackled the big ham steak and pile of fried potatoes, it was all he could do to pretend nothing unusual was going on. His father gave him nary a glance that told him they shared a secret. As Eben ate, he listened to his parents' conversation. Slowly, he began to realize that they were talking about unimportant things. There was not a word said about the war. They were simply making talk. Stopping his laden fork midway to his mouth, it came to Eben that his mother knew of the work he and his father would do this night. He chewed his meat slowly, watching her with mounting pride. There was no nervousness that he could detect. She knew what had to be done and she accepted the fact that her son and husband were the best qualified to do it.

Even when he and his father left the house at eight o'clock, Amanda Tyne acted as if nothing unusual was happening, except that she gave each of them a long, silent embrace as they stepped from the back door and Captain Tyne shut it behind him. Looking back at the house, Eben saw her watching them from between parted parlor draperies. Light from the coal-oil lamp in her hand showed her face ghost-white. He could see the strain in it as she suddenly pulled the blue velvet portieres closed. To Eben, her gesture had been almost an angry one. But why?

The waters at dockside were pitch-black. Not even a reflected light touched the *Lucy*'s hull. Her four-man crew spoke in whispers as her bow and stern lines were cast off. A good push with an oar from the dock sent the launch out into the Elizabeth River, where she began to drift with the ebbing tide.

"We're in the ebb now," Mr. Wharton murmured softly. "We all know how sound carries over water, so don't anybody talk. In a few minutes, we'll start to row. Be sure the oar's blade goes in clean and that it's pulled out clean. Just one noisy one and we could be done for. Steam's up in the boiler if we need it, but it's to be slow and easy for now. Eben, you take the bow oar here on the port side. I'll have the stern one. Your father and Mr. Stanley will row the starboard side. If we're hailed, Eben, you shout out right away that we're a fishing boat. Any questions, lad?"

"No, Sir, aye, Sir," Eben answered as sailors had for hundreds of years. He was a good oarsman, and he knew there wouldn't be any splashed water from sloppy oar handling on his part.

He walked to the bow, positioned his oar so that it hung out well above the sullen, cold blackness below it, and sat waiting. At the soft call from Wharton, he dipped the oar and pushed against its long handle as it moved in its cloth-wrapped oarlock. As quiet as winter fog came in, the *Lucy* moved toward the Yankee fleet. The mission had begun!

After fifteen minutes of silent rowing, Wharton whispered, "In oars," and they were brought on board again and very carefully placed on the deck. The *Lucy* had arrived at mid-channel, where the torpedoes were to be set.

"Eben," whispered Captain Tyne, who was just a darker shape in the darkness, "keep a good lookout. Your young eyes and ears are the sharpest. We're ready to set the first group of torpedoes."

Sitting as still as his mother's chinaware spaniels on the parlor mantel, Eben strained to see and to hear. All he caught was a series of soft gurglings from the water at the *Lucy*'s stern as the clay pots were anchored some fifteen feet apart while she drifted. The torpedoes would stay afloat just under the bay's surface.

Then, at a low-toned command from Mr. Wharton, the slow rowing began once more. Two more sets of torpedoes were anchored as the launch moved down the channel toward the Yankee ships.

When the *Lucy* reached the spot where the channel turned to flow to the sea, she moved more rapidly, drifting with the current into deeper waters, parallel to the line of blockading frigates. Silently, she drifted, now too close to them to risk using her oars. The only sound that Eben could hear was that of a dog barking from the shore. As he tried to pinpoint the dog's location, the sound of ship's bells on the Yankee blockaders told him the hour of the watch—the hours of the night. Six bells rang. That meant it was eleven o'clock, and they'd been out on the bay for two hours. It also meant that it wasn't long before slack-water time, when the tide would change from ebb flow to flood. Then the *Lucy*'s course would be reversed and she'd drift silently back toward her home port and away from the threat of the Yankee ships' guns.

The fourth set of torpedoes had just been slipped into the bay in the deeper reach of the channel, and the fifth set was being readied to be set, too, when the sudden throbbing of an engine came to Eben's ears. It sounded from the seaward side. Eben tensed, every muscle taut. He knew this would be a Yankee ship.

There wouldn't be time to set the last torpedoes. The *Lucy* had to run. Run right now! Noiselessly, the remaining torpedoes were jettisoned overboard into the bay. Quietly, more wood was set into the *Lucy*'s firebox to keep her steam up. Silently, the four sailors aboard her waited, listening.

The direction of the sound let Eben know the steamer was in the channel and coming directly toward the *Lucy*. Her noises made him think that she had an underwater propeller. That alone would make her much faster and easier to handle than the little side-wheeler. He knew they would be lucky to get away from the Yankees in time.

Captain Tyne gave an order to take up the oars. Eben knew that he hoped to get the *Lucy* out of the channel and into shallower waters, where she would be to one side of the oncoming vessel rather than directly in front of her. As the men began to stroke, the *Lucy* seemed to move faster than she had before for them. Even with their hard rowing, however, the sounds of the approaching steamer got louder and louder as the other ship came nearer.

Now Captain Tyne ordered, "Stop rowing! Ready with the steam! Lash everything down and find a spot where you can get some protection if the Yankees fire on us. Eben, you stay with me by the helm to answer any hail. Once you've replied, go to the engine room and start piling on wood. Mr. Wharton, you're the engineer and will man the boiler. Mr. Stanley, stand ready to take care of any damage done. If we're found out, we'll make a run for the beach by the Rip Raps. They won't expect us to do that. We'll have a good enough chance! To your duties, men!"

Eben was astonished at what his father had just said. The Rip Raps where the waters shoaled were a long mile away and on the other side of the vessel that was bearing down on them. They would have to pass across the Yankees' bow to get there. Then suddenly, he saw the wisdom of the plan. It would seem that the *Lucy* was going away from, not toward, Norfolk. In the dark night, it could be mistaken for a Union ship. Even if she was not, the larger enemy steamer would have to come about to chase her. The time it took the Yankees to turn in a narrow channel would give the *Lucy* a few more minutes, which could make all the difference between death or capture or freedom.

It wasn't three minutes later that the lookout on the approaching ship called out to the *Lucy:* "This is the U.S.S. gunboat *Shrike.* Who are you?"

Eben called back, surprised at the firmness of his voice when he himself was trembling. "Ahoy, *Shrike.* This is the crabber *Lucy.*"

A minute passed, then came a second hail. "Lay to, *Lucy,* to be boarded and searched. You're under our guns."

"Mr. Wharton, kick on the steam," called Captain Tyne through the speaking tube to the engine room. As the *Lucy*'s paddle wheels began to move, Sam Tyne ordered his son: "Hail them and ask if they said 'Come to you.' Pretend you didn't get their message right."

"Stand by, *Shrike,*" yelled Eben, trying to drown out any noises the *Lucy* was now making. "I'm coming to you."

"Avast that! Lay to!" was the reply.

Over the splashing of the paddle wheels, Eben called back, "What'd that be? I don't hear you so well."

"Lay to, I say, or we shoot!"

Now, Eben heard the metallic sounds of the *Shrike*'s gun crew begin to aim their cannons at the *Lucy*.

"I can't hear you! I'm coming closer!" shouted Eben even louder while his father pointed the *Lucy* toward the Rip Raps. If the *Shrike* hesitated in firing just a bit, there would be a chance for the paddle wheels.

The next shout from the Yankee was a roar of anger. "Lay to or we'll blow you out of the water!"

As Sam Tyne hastily steered the *Lucy*'s bow closer to the beach, Eben called to the Yankee, cupping his hands to his mouth: "Be this what you want? I still can't hear you well."

The minute he had finished his words, he heard his father's warning voice. "Steady, son. Don't call out to 'em anymore. We're played out. Be off to the engine room. I want all the steam I can get. Stoke the boiler. You're a fine shipmate—the best. Off with you!"

As Eben moved to go below, he saw his father spin the wheel another two spokes to the starboard to close the distance to the shore. He knew they had played the Yankees for time and had gained a few precious minutes. Every yard they traveled without enemy cannon blasting at them was vital now. They had to trust to luck.

The paddle-wheeler was aimed at the shoal water just ahead when a tremendous splash appeared suddenly just beneath her bow. Frothing water was thrown high into the air, and the sulfur smell of gunpowder enveloped the *Lucy* as the two reports—one from the explosion and the other from the cannonball itself—came crashing through the air. Midway to the engine room, Eben Tyne hit the deck. There wasn't any fine adventure in being shot at by a cannon. Then he was up and ran back to the helm. He had to make sure his father was all right!

Relief surged through him as he caught sight of his father's shape still at the helm. Sam Tyne told him, "That was only a shot across our bow. It's the navy's way of telling us to heave to or be sunk. I think we've got maybe a minute before they shoot to try to hit us next time. I'll slip this loop of rope over the spoke of the wheel and we'll both go to the engine room. The *Lucy*'s set on her course. We ought to be safe belowdecks. Lively now, Eben; we're in the war, it seems."

With one swift movement, the rope was flung over the spoke and the *Lucy* headed for the beach with no helmsman at her wheel. Running along her deck, the Tynes rushed into the engine room to join Wharton and Stanley. Father and son had just reached the bottom of the ladder by the stack of firewood when there came a very sharp explosion just above them on the deck. *Crack!*

"It's the cabin that's been hit," cried Captain Tyne.

Another two minutes passed as the crew furiously restacked the firewood to make a barricade to protect themselves. Then came another crash of an exploding shell. This time, Eben's father called out that the *Lucy*'s wheelhouse had taken a direct hit. If only her rudder stayed pointed true to the shore. Eben prayed as fervently as he so recently had prayed to find Jason in the water, and he prayed with his eyes fixed on the steam-making fire burning in the boiler.

The third Yankee shot was the worst of all. A crashing roar to the left of the engine room told Eben that the paddle-wheel housing had flown into the air. Badly damaged in her port wheel, the *Lucy* would now steam in circles because her starboard wheel would have a greater push to move her hull.

Stanley, the carpenter, was on his feet and at the ladder at once, climbing the rungs to get on deck to make as many repairs as he could to correct the *Lucy*'s course. However, as he stepped out onto the deck, he was blown right back down into the engine room by another Yankee shot. He landed unconscious on the oak logs, bleeding at his head and with one leg twisted oddly under him. This time, the starboard paddle wheel had been hit! The *Lucy*'s movement to the beach was now rough and uneven. To Eben, her paddling sounded like the old church organ at home when it was played without being fully pumped up.

As Mr. Wharton opened the steam valve of the engine to get the fullest speed possible, Captain Tyne examined Stanley. Eben watched by the red light of the fire as his father knelt beside the carpenter to get his pulse.

Captain Tyne said hoarsely, "He's got a broken leg and a cut on his head. He's not dying, lad." Suddenly, to Eben's amazement, his father chuckled and added, "We are a little safer now. That last shot evened up the paddle wheels. We'll be slower, but most likely we'll stay on course for the beach, and—"

He never finished his sentence. Father and son were thrown to the engine room's deck in a heap of arms and legs. A solid shot had hit the *Lucy*'s stern, gone through her cargo hold and bulkheads, and ended up tossing the heavy oak cordwood about as if the logs had been twigs.

This was too much, thought Eben, anger against the enemy now overpowering his fear. Picking himself up from beneath three logs that were scattered over his legs, Eben looked first at his father and then at Mr. Wharton, who'd been feeding the firebox. Both men were covered with logs and both were unconscious. The engineer was moaning. With no thought for himself, Eben began throwing the heavy wood away from the men. After freeing them, he crouched low as another solid shot from the *Shrike* ripped through the *Lucy*'s hull, barely missing her boiler. Had the shot struck it, all four of them would have been killed by its superheated steam—boiled alive. Eben knew how lucky they had just been.

Eben dragged his father behind the engine housing. He made a second trip to get Mr. Wharton there also. As Eben was about to go for Mr. Stanley, another shot struck the bow of the *Lucy* and knocked him off his feet. He struggled up, then tugged the carpenter to the protection of the engine mount. Not knowing what else to do, and frustrated by his helplessness, Eben dipped a nearby rag into the bilge water and bathed his father's forehead. He talked to him but got no answer.

Redampening the cloth, he did the same for the other men. As he bent over Stanley, he saw to his horror that water was coming up over one end of the engine room's deck boards.

The *Lucy* was sinking.

It was up to him, Eben Tyne, to get her to shore. If the paddle-wheeler sank before he could, he might lose his father and the other two men.

Eben frantically started stoking the firebox with oak. Steam! He had to have *steam* to get the crippled boat to the shoals before she sank under them!

Log in hand and the firebox open, he was thrown to the deck again by the next cannon shot. This time, it had the crashing sound of an explosive and he was aware of a "tinny" taste in his mouth. He felt as if a club had hit him on the head. Getting to his feet, Eben saw that the afterdeck was gone. Now he could look right up to the night stars from where he stood in the engine room. One more hit like that one and the *Lucy* would be a complete wreck. The Yankees were good cannoneers. If they did this well in the dark, how would they do in daylight?

Eben dismissed the thought and turned his mind to the little ship. Only her courage and his own were keeping her afloat at all as she struggled on, sinking ever more deeply into the water, but still gallantly heading toward the shore.

Right now, his father and the other men were not only in danger of being killed by enemy fire but in peril of drowning from the water coming in through the holes in the *Lucy*'s hull. Eben hurried to his father and raised him to a sitting position. Then he propped up Wharton and the carpenter beside him. Placing his own body between the injured men and the cannon fire, Eben waited for the next shot, which was sure to come at any second.

He was able to hold the men away from the incoming seas for a few seconds only. When the next shot came, all four of them were tossed forward like one of Becky's old rag dolls, to collide with the engine-room bulkhead.

There came next a rending crash and a sudden tilt to the deck, accompanied by a cloud of hissing steam that filled the engine room.

Had the boiler blown up? No, her boiler safety valve had popped off at this grinding impact, so her boiler had released steam. The crash came because the *Lucy* had reached the shoals! She had piled up on them. Now the paddle-wheeler couldn't sink, because she was in shallow water.

She could still be pounded to pieces by the Federal ship's cannons, however!

In the sudden stillness after the ship had come aground, Eben heard more noises of explosions. These were deeper-sounding than before, and near. They were not hitting the stranded *Lucy*, though. They weren't aimed at her. These shots were going over her and landing out in the bay—aimed at the *Shrike*.

Eben's heart lifted. This was firing from the Confederate cannons on shore. They would stop the Yankee gunboat's firing and drive her into waters that would be out of the *Lucy*'s range.

When the shore guns finally fell silent, Eben sat down suddenly as his legs gave way under him. He was shaking uncontrollably. His nerves, tight as steel during the extreme danger, vibrated as they had not once done aboard the *Sarah* in the squall. His mind told him how very close to dying he had come just now. He had known war.

Controlling himself by sheer will and by an ever-mounting anger at the Yankees, Eben gritted his teeth to keep them from chattering and he looked around at his stranded ship. By now, his eyes were accustomed enough to the darkness to let him see that the *Lucy* was one mass of wreckage. One glance over the side at the rocks below her showed him there was no way for him to refloat her. He spent less than thirty seconds making up his mind. He must get everyone off the *Lucy* before the tide changed and she was lifted off the rocks, took on water, and sank.

There was only one thing he could do. He turned to the three men with determination. Grasping them under their arms, he pulled them, one after the other, up onto the deck, where he laid them flat in a row. Then, gathering up long planks that had been part of the deckhouse, he hurriedly lashed the planks together with pieces of rope to make a crude raft. Splinters drove themselves into his hands, but he never felt them. Pushing with all his strength, he launched his raft over the submerged stern of the paddle-wheeler. It floated freely. He pushed and tugged the men aboard the crude raft, once nearly sinking it, but finally all three were aboard, with their heads well up out of the water.

Swimming hard, the need for haste giving him surprising strength, Eben Tyne pushed the raft in front of him and made for the shore. How badly had his father been hurt? What of the other two? Time and time again, Eben stopped swimming so that he could reach over and touch the chests of the three men to see that they still breathed. He didn't know how to give them the help they needed. The best thing he could do was push for the shore as fast as he could. His mind focused only on swimming and getting the raft to the beach.

All at once, he touched bottom with a toe as he kicked.

At the same moment, hands reached to him and he was pulled up onto the cold sand. Then, standing dripping and chilled, Eben watched as the raft was lifted bodily from the water. Dark figures stood all around.

Suddenly, from down in Norfolk Bay's channel came the noise of a tremendous explosion. Eben knew at once what had caused it. The *Shrike* had found one of the *Lucy*'s torpedoes!

"Your work?" came the question from one of the men near him. The voice was that of a Virginian, softly Southern.

"Aye, Sir. It was one of the torpedoes we set tonight. These men are hurt. One's my father. The other two are off the *Zephyr*."

"We have a doctor. He's coming," replied the same voice as the raft and its passengers were lifted by eight men. The Virginian now asked, "Who are you and why are you here?"

"Eben Tyne, from Norfolk, Sir. That's my name. The *Lucy* was my ship."

The man said, "The little paddle-wheeler, huh? I'm

Major Wellesley, Norfolk Light Artillery. We were the ones firing on that ship that just now took your torpedo."

Eben told him, "She was the *Shrike,* Sir." He looked not at the soldier but at the raft, where a coal-oil lamp had just been lit and set in the sand.

A deeper voice from one of the Confederates who had knelt to attend the wounded said, "They're all breathing all right, Sir. One's got a busted leg, I think, and there's some bleedin'. Far as I can tell, that's all that's wrong."

"Good. The doctor should be here presently. He was told to come to the beach. I expected injuries when I saw the raft coming in."

Eben told the officer, "My pa's Captain Samuel Tyne. He's the tall one on the raft there."

"Captain Tyne? I've heard of him." The major volunteered, "My home's in Newport News, across the bay. Your father's name is well known there." Going over to peer closely at Sam Tyne's face, the major went on. "It's my guess he's senseless from concussion from all that firing. It's common. He'll probably come to after a while. About your ship, lad. Even though she's been wrecked, she's still valuable and we'll try to salvage her. The South needs every ship it's got. We can try to take her engine out and get her refloated at high tide. Then we can tow her back to Norfolk behind another boat at night. Maybe she'll be back in service inside the month and you can go out on her again."

Again? Eben looked at the silent, dark water and trembled—partly from the night chill and partly from what he'd just gone through.

He heard Mr. Wharton groan now and went to squat beside him. The engineer took a deep breath and sat up, blinking at his unknown surroundings. He stared wordlessly, his eyes focusing on the army officer beside Eben. A look of relief lit up his face as he saw the gray uniform in the lamp's glow. Eben read Wharton's thoughts. No, he wasn't a Yankee prisoner! The first mate got up and slowly bent over the other two men from the *Lucy*. He placed his hand on the forehead of each man, then put the back of his hand on the neck of each to feel for a throb of pulse. Satisfied, he let out a long, slow breath and was about to speak when a little white-bearded man arrived at a quick walk.

He went first to Mr. Wharton, who waved him off, showing he could stand up and was all right. He gestured to his shipmates.

"The man to the left, Doctor," the Confederate major broke in sharply. "He has a broken leg. He's been moving some. The other one, Captain Tyne, has been still. He's breathing, but that's all we can tell about him."

Eben held his breath. Was his father badly hurt?

• 59 •

He watched in fear as the doctor ordered the soldiers around the *Zephyr*'s carpenter. "You, Corporal, cut the pants away from that broken leg, but don't move it. You others, get me some strong flat sticks for splints. I'll be right there."

As he opened the black leather bag of instruments and medicines he had with him, he hurried to Eben's father. He knelt and made a quick inspection, pulling up Sam Tyne's eyelids. Saying nothing, he took a small dark bottle from his bag, jerked out its cork, and held it under the captain's nose. Eben watched intently as the sharp, foul order of smelling salts caused a swift movement of his father's head as he tried to get away from the offensive sting and smell that followed his nose each time he moved. Satisfied, the doctor corked the bottle, then looked up at the major and Eben and said, "I'd say it's simple concussion. His color's good even in this accursed light. But he'll have a headache like he got kicked by a horse when he comes to, which will be any minute now."

Next, the doctor turned to Mr. Stanley, who was moaning. Working swiftly and expertly, the doctor pulled the broken leg straight and the thighbone into line by feel. Then he applied the splints and bandages to the leg.

"Now, that's done," he said, mostly to himself, as he got up and stared at Eben's father, who was moving his arms and legs by now. He continued: "It's lucky that man stayed unconscious while I set his leg. It would've been mighty painful when we stretched the leg muscles. He can go home in a wagon, and the leg will heal naturally. I'll see that he gets some laudanum for the pain. A couple cups of strong coffee will fix the other two up."

Suddenly, he stopped talking and stared at Eben, then crooked a finger at him and said, "Boy, let's see that leg of yours. You're bleeding!"

Surprised, Eben looked down at his legs. His left pant leg was bloody at the knee. Pulling up the pants, he saw a large bruise just above his knee and a jagged cut in its center. He hadn't even known it was there. When had that happened?

The little doctor chuckled and said, "You didn't feel it, did you? Well, that happens in wartime. You get too excited for pain. Now, let's have a look at that leg." Bent over to examine it, the doctor went on, "You're lucky the bay's saltwater. That cleans wounds very well. A touch of alcohol will wash the cut out, but I think you're going to have to have two stitches at least. Sewing you up'll hurt, but I bet you're brave enough to stand that, aren't you, boy?"

Eben tried not to tremble. Being sewed up would hurt, but the doctor said he had to be sewed. He bit his lip. "Go on," said Eben. "Do what you need to do."

After rummaging a bit in his bag, the doctor pulled

out another small bottle. He took a curved needle from it that was already threaded with white catgut soaked in alcohol.

He told Eben, "This will hurt like fury; I won't tell you otherwise. Soldier, bring that lantern closer so I can see better." Once more, the doctor knelt. "Are you ready, son?"

"Aye, sir." While the doctor swabbed and stitched, Eben stared up unblinking into the major's sympathetic face. The man was right—it did hurt like fury, and he had to force himself not to cry out or jerk away as the needle was passed through the wound. Finally, the last piece of catgut was tied and the wound was bandaged.

When the doctor was through, he muttered with a grin of approval. "Young man, you're a chesty fellow. I wouldn't mind having you as one of my own boys, as a matter of fact. You didn't even wince much at all."

"Thank you, sir," Eben said simply, and asked, "How's my pa?"

The major answered him. "If you look over there, son, you'll see he's got up and found a log to sit on. He's sort of shaky, I reckon, or he'd be over here with you. He hasn't taken his eyes off you one time."

Eben turned his head to where the officer pointed. Yes, both Captain Tyne and Mr. Wharton were seated on a log. Thank the Lord, they were both all right, too. His father nodded gravely at him, then nodded again.

Now Major Wellesley told the men milling around, "We have some hot coffee over the hill." He pointed to the sand dune just behind him. "Let's go get some. The man with the broken leg will stay here. Don't try to pick him up. We'll send a wagon to collect him shortly."

"I'll stay here, Major," said the doctor, "to see that my patient is loaded on the wagon properly, not like a sack of oats. Then I'll come join you."

Slowly, with soldiers supporting both Mr. Wharton and Captain Tyne, they all started over the sand to the battery position of the Norfolk Light Artillery. At first, Eben walked with the comforting hand of the major under his elbow, but eventually that was replaced by his father's. Eben knew this wasn't just support for his bad knee, but approval as well. He had proved himself just fine.

CHAPTER FOUR

NEW DUTIES?

It was near sunup when the carpenter had been taken safely home, the first mate of the *Zephyr* had returned to his ship, and the two Tynes entered their house. Though Amanda Tyne looked composed as she met them at the door, Eben guessed she had sat up all night listening, straining her ears to catch every sound from the bay. She must have heard the many loud explosions and been frightened. It was too bad that she had had so much worry, but wartime was a worrisome time for everyone. She ought to know that, too.

Although Captain Tyne and Eben didn't lie to her

about their injuries or the night's events, they did not give her every detail, either. Whether she knew they were holding back so as not to worry her further, Eben was not sure. He did, however, know that Amanda Tyne was the daughter and wife of seafaring men. She had lived all her life with the uncertainties brought by the sea.

After eating the filling snack his mother hastily prepared, Eben climbed the steep stairs and slid into his bed. He tried to fall asleep, but sleep would not come. Mentally, he relived his time in the engine room of the *Lucy*. He knew he had done well—both his father and Major Wellesley had said so. He was a sailor! He'd done what any good sailor would do. But he'd been lucky, too. Thinking of the firing from the *Shrike* made him shudder even now. Would he do as well in battle the next time—if there was to be a next time? Lord, let him act as bravely!

Kicking off the muslin sheet covering him, he stretched out, felt his throbbing leg, and touched the bandages to see they were not loose. He lay back, closed his eyes, and finally drifted into a sleep of weariness.

It was nearly ten when Eben awoke. He had been asleep for five hours. Wincing as he stood, he moved his leg to ease the stiffness. Then he washed his face, neck, and shoulders in his washbasin. Finally, he got into clean overalls and the blue-checked cotton shirt his mother had set out for him atop his sea chest, and went down to the kitchen. Surprised, he saw that the woodbox was full and the stove ashes had been raked out of the stove into a bucket. Sam Tyne had done his son's chores. This was something new and different. Eben was surprised.

At the stove, preparing Eben's customary breakfast of bacon and hot corn bread, Amanda Tyne said quietly, "Your father says you did very well last night, Eben."

"Where is he?" asked the boy.

"Gone to the *Zephyr* in spite of his headache. He refused to sleep late today." Mrs. Tyne shook her head as she came to the table with the heavy iron pan in which she'd baked the corn bread.

Eben told her, "I'll eat up fast and then be on my way to school."

His mother stood, pan in hand, her face hardening. "Oh, no, you won't! You can stay home for one day and keep off that leg of yours. Just because your father feels he has to do something bad for his health doesn't mean that you have to, too. You rest here."

"But, Ma, what about my homework assignments?"

"You can go over to see Jason this afternoon and get them from him."

"But I want to go to school. I feel just fine."

"I don't care what you say. I won't permit you to get overtired and sick. You don't want your leg infected, do you?"

Seeing how adamant his mother was, Eben submitted with a growl. "Oh, all right." He reckoned he'd go sit out in the sunshine after breakfast and whittle till school was out and Jason had come home.

Later that day, as Eben sat at the kitchen table with his leg propped up on a chair seat, his father walked into the house.

"I've been down to the *Zephyr*," he told his son. "Captain Walter and Mr. Wharton are coming here later on today. They'll be having supper with us, but it's you they want to see. Captain Walter has something for you. Our carpenter shipmate is doing fine. I saw him, too. He sends his best."

Eben stared at his father in surprise. Captain Walter coming to see him? Coming to give him something? What could that be?

Lost in these thoughts, Eben heard his father's next words but didn't pay close heed to them until the captain said, "Then Jason's father and I will be leaving the day after tomorrow to get our ship for France. You'll be the man of the house here, Eben, at least for a while. And I also have to tell you that it's just been decided that your friend Jason will be sailing with us."

"*Jason?* Jason's going with you? To France? Why not me?" Eben blurted. Anger and envy suddenly caught at him. He'd been the one who had proved his worth the previous night. Jason had not.

"There's other work for you to do here," his father continued, "and Jason's father may have need of an apprentice engineer who is small enough to get back into the crannies of an engine room where a full-size man cannot go while the ship is under way. As you know, Jason Owens is nimble and can bend in any direction. He's just the person who might save a crippled ship someday in the middle of the ocean. You are not."

Eben was stung by his father's words. Hadn't he brought the crippled *Lucy* safely to shore? Her crew might well owe him their lives. Surely that counted for something.

Captain Tyne sat down facing his resentful son. The silence seemed long before he spoke again. "Now, Eben, let's talk about *your* future! I went to visit your teacher after I left Mr. Stanley's sickbed. I told Miss Mitchell that you might be leaving school for a while."

"*Leaving* school, Pa?"

"Yes, there's been a lot of talk during the last few hours about what you did on the *Lucy* in saving our lives." Again there was silence, then he said, "This is a crucial time for the South. She needs every good man she can muster, both the young and the old. Jason will go with us because he can do the most good on our voyage. You, if you agree, will go to work on the new warship that is being built over in the Gosport Navy Yard."

Eben said excitedly, "The new ship that we aren't supposed to talk about? *Me?*"

"Aye, that's right, the secret ship. She'll be the most unusual vessel ever built and won't have to count on sails for power. Her mission is to break the Union blockade and open the sea-lanes to Europe for the Southern merchant ships so we can get our cotton sold."

Now as delighted as he had been disappointed a few minutes before, Eben asked, "Why do they want *me,* and why all of a sudden?"

"Why you? Well, while I was aboard the *Zephyr* this morning, a young officer from that secret ship came looking for me. He's her second-in-command. His name is Lieutenant Catesby ap Jones. He'd heard all about the doings aboard the *Lucy* last night . . . most likely from the army major who fished us all out of the water. Jones asked me if you would want to join his ship. He's heard you've got plenty of grit and admires that in a lad. He's making up a crew. I told him I'd ask you, but the decision is yours alone, Eben."

To join a ship's crew—a warship's crew? Eben's eyes blazed with excitement.

Captain Tyne went on. "Eben, there could be danger. You're just a lad yet, but brave men on both sides are going to have to pay the price of this war, like they do in all wars. People are willing to fight and die for what they value, but only a fool would enjoy war. This is why we've got to end this one as fast as we can with as few losses in lives as possible. As I say, you could find danger, and to join a ship is your decision alone."

"Pa, I know that. What's the ship?" Eben asked.

"The *Merrimack*. Remember when she came to Norfolk about a year ago to be repaired? She was one of the finest and best steam frigates of the Yankee navy. You and I talked about her then, wondering what would happen if a war came. Her engines needed work, and the Yankees didn't have time to move her out when they abandoned the yard to us. They set fire to her, and she was burned to her waterline and sank at her dock. But the South has refloated her and is keeping her pretty much secret." As if to emphasize his next words, Captain Tyne lowered his voice. "There are spies everywhere these days, son. Even with all our secrecy, the North might know the U.S.S. *Merrimack* is being rebuilt into an ironclad, a ship that is covered with iron plates that will protect her from cannonballs. We've renamed her the Confederate States Ship *Virginia*."

Eben sucked in his breath. An ironclad ship? There had never been such a vessel before. He wanted to go to Gosport that very minute, but he knew he could not. His father continued. "Today and tomorrow, you'll most likely help Jason get ready to sail with us. Later, we'll need to discuss the things here you have to know about while I'm gone. Just rest your leg today. Tomorrow, you and I will take the rowboat across the river to the navy yard and have a look at your new ship. How does that sound to you?"

"Fine, Pa. Does Ma know?"

"Not yet. I'm going to tell her now. I think she'll understand. She doesn't expect us not to have to make sacrifices in wartime. She won't be glad to have you aboard the *Merrimack,* but you shouldn't be in any danger there. I'll tell her that. The *Merrimack*'s armor will make any hits bounce off. If I didn't think you'd be all right, I wouldn't let you go. You know that without being told. You'll be home with her nights. I'll go upstairs now and talk with her."

Not ten minutes later, while Eben thought of the *Merrimack* and joyously anticipated going aboard her, Jason came running into the Tyne house, his eyes gleaming. As he settled himself onto a straight-backed chair, he cried, "I'm off to seek the Ring-Dang-Doo, Eben," using the sailor's slang to indicate a place very far away.

Excitedly, the two boys compared notes, each happy for the other's good fortune but secretly wishing that they could go together either to France or to serve on the secret ship. They had never pursued such separate interests before.

Jason spoke of what he was to learn about engines on the ship to Le Havre. By the end of the voyage, he would know how steam engines worked by tending them and sometimes moving about inside them.

Then it was Eben's turn to repeat everything his

father had told him about the *Merrimack.* He also told him about his adventures aboard the *Lucy* and showed him his bad leg. To prove he wasn't badly hurt, Eben got up and walked around, bending and stretching as naturally as he could—not showing that it hurt plenty.

Time raced as the two friends talked of their futures, and it seemed but minutes before Jason had to go back to his own home, although they had spent a full hour in excited talk.

It didn't occur to Eben that his father and mother had not come downstairs nor that there had been no sounds from above. When Captain Tyne finally did come clumping down, he went outside to light his pipe without saying a word to his son. His face was somber. Eben reckoned he must be thinking of the voyage to France and its dangers in wartime.

The visit of the *Zephyr's* master and first mate was one Eben would long remember. The men arrived shortly before five o'clock. Eben saw at once that Captain Walter carried a small wrapped package under his thick arm. The boy knew it was for him—it was the "something" of which his father had spoken. Wordlessly, the captain unwrapped the brown paper and gave Eben a little box wrapped in bright scarlet Peking paper. As Eben took it, Mr. Wharton told him the gift was accompanied by the thanks of all his shipmates on the clipper.

At first, Eben tried politely to decline the gift and return it to the old captain, saying he'd only done his duty as a sailor and a Southerner. Captain Walter only shook his head. So now Eben took the paper from the package, to find a carved rosewood box with brass-bound corners and the ivory inlay of a Chinese junk under full sail on its lid. The brass padlock was oddly shaped, very like a tiny metal miniature of a doctor's bag. Clearly this box had been a precious treasure of Captain Marcus Walter for some time.

Eben offered the box back to the old sea captain, shaking his head to say he couldn't accept so grand a gift.

Captain Walter looked amused, then he laughed aloud, booming laugh. "Nonsense, boy. It's yours! Open it up. Here is the key." And he produced the tiny key from the pocket of his watch coat.

Eben found the key slid easily into the lock. In an instant, the box was opened and its lid flipped up. A sweet perfume came from it, the smell of the sandalwood that lined its interior. At the bottom of the box, nestled in a wrapping of white silk, was a gold pocket watch with a snap cover to protect its face from scratches and the weather. Gazing in delight at its dial with Roman numeral letters, Eben saw that there was a thin gold ring around the watch and four tiny brass projections inside the box. It was not a watch at all! It was much more important than that.

It was a ship's chronometer that would time the sun and moon for navigation. It could be mounted between the brass projections by its ring and would always hang level, even if the ship was rolling and tossing in high seas. It was a wondrous instrument—and far too costly for the likes of him to own.

When Eben offered the box to Captain Walter a third time, the man took it. Grinning, he placed it on top of the parlor mantel and gave it a pat with his brown hand, saying, "That's that! It's yours. Maybe someday you'll use this aboard your own ship. Now, Mistress Tyne, that's a mouth-watering smell coming from your kitchen."

Eben's mother told him, "When we have guests, Captain, we make a special effort for their comfort and pleasure." She nodded and went to the kitchen, but without giving the captain a wide smile as Eben would have expected her to do.

Again a delicious dinner of yellow corned ham and hominy came from his mother's hours in the kitchen. It was served up to a lively conversation among the men and Eben. For the first time in his life, the boy felt himself a guest of honor. Any question he asked was answered in full, something that was a complete change from being at the table as a child and speaking only when he was spoken to. By the time the whipped cream and cherry preserves pie came along as dessert, Eben knew he had won himself a spot as a cabin boy and officer-trainee on board the *Zephyr* when the war was ended. He could never ask for better men under whom to train.

Dinner over, Mrs. Tyne left the table. Eben's father and Mr. Wharton lit up cigars, while Captain Walter's briar pipe peeked out from his iron-colored whiskers. Now the talk turned to the *Merrimack*. It was the first time this topic had ever been talked about in front of Eben. The three men knew the facts and discussed them so that Eben would be knowledgeable of his ship before he joined her. As he listened, he was startled to hear that the *Merrimack*'s deck was only two feet above her gigantic seventeen-foot propeller.

Eben exploded, "Why, she'll sit like a plank in the water!"

The *Zephyr*'s master pulled his pipe from his mouth. Using its stem as if he were writing in air, he explained, "Aye, she's been cut down so far, she can only serve in flat water. Any seas or surf and it will be Davy Jones's locker for her—she will sink to the bottom. But that doesn't matter. Norfolk Bay's where this ship will make her name on a calm day, God willing. It's up to her to uncork that plug out in the bay—the Union frigates. The main problem as I see it"—he took several puffs from his pipe and continued speaking from behind a gray cloud—"is for her to move freely. She will float twenty-two feet, and the channel is only twenty-four feet at low tide. Yet, if she isn't in the channel, she'll go upon the shoals, where there are all kinds of mud banks to trap her." He concluded by saying, "If she gets hung on a bar, she'll be in trouble, because her engines are in poor shape."

"That could well be, Captain," said his first mate, "but there's nothing afloat in the bay that can exchange cannon shots with the *Merrimack* without getting sunk. She's an ironclad. Yankee cannonballs will bounce off her plating, while her cannon shots will go right through the wooden hulls of the frigates out there."

Captain Tyne was speaking now. "The fight between our ironclad and the Yankee blockaders is going to be hard, but the *Merrimack* ought to win it. No wooden vessel will be able to stand against her. She'll break the blockade here, and our ships will be back on the ocean where they belong. But the steam-driven ship is going to ring down the curtain on us old wind sailors, and the armor-plated gunboat will spell the end of the wood-hulled warships. The men who crew these new ships won't be sail-furling, rope-splicing sailors like us. These new ships will need blacksmiths, machinists, boilermakers, mechanics, and officers who'll be engineers more than they will be seamen. Aye, I say that sail will gradually disappear from the sea, and I hate to see it happen."

Eben agreed. He loved the splendor of sail and

didn't want to see it go. He asked, "How long will it take before there's nothing afloat but steamships, Pa?"

"That's hard to say. I'd guess sail will stay strong for twenty, thirty years more. By then, engines will be better. There'll come the day when regular schedules of sailings and arrivals will be common, not like today where the winds order our speed and our course and can give us fast voyages or slow ones." He let out a sigh. "Times change and people have to change with them, but there is nothing more difficult than change."

Eben frowned. He wanted nothing to do with engine rooms after his night in the *Lucy*. Let Jason have engines! On a big ship, there would be steam pipes all over—hot boilers and men stoking coal into the fireboxes to make the steam. There would be no stirring winds to ruffle a person's hair and nothing to see but what was in the dingy engine room belowdecks. What real sailor would want that? Not he. No, sir, he told himself. He'd rather serve up on the deck where the fighting would be, not in any engine room. He would do better to serve as a cannoneer than throw wood and coal into fireboxes.

He said, "The *Merrimack*'ll have to carry big guns to fight the Yankees, won't she? That's where I want to be. But maybe I'm not big enough and strong enough yet to carry cannonballs."

Captain Tyne explained, "Yes, Eben, it was cannon that Lieutenant Jones of the *Merrimack* had in mind for you eventually. He said he thought from what he'd heard that you'd have the makings of a powder-monkey. That's the lad who takes the gunpowder up to the cannon from the ship's hold. Serving the guns is an important job."

"That's the job for me, then, Pa. I want to serve the *Merrimack*'s guns."

Captain Walter laughed and boomed, "Bravo, lad. Mr. Wharton, it's time we went back to our ship." He thanked Eben's mother at the door for her fine meal and the hospitality of her home and bowed. Then the two mariners started back to their never-ending task of keeping the *Zephyr* ready to break for the open sea at a moment's orders.

After they left, Eben walked to the barn, milked the cow, and did his evening chores, not forgetting to put down milk for the family's cat, Napoleon. Then he went to his room, picked up his battered copy of *Ivanhoe,* and read of knights and their noble deeds until he felt sleepy. With his father leaving so soon, he wanted his parents to have as much time together in private as possible. At the same time, however, he sensed something was wrong between them.

CHAPTER FIVE

THE "SECRET" SHIP

"*Merrimack* Day," Eben told himself as he got out of bed at first daylight. Feeling almost no pain in his leg by now, only a stiffness, he attended to his morning chores. After breakfast, he walked with his father to the main dock on the Elizabeth River. When they arrived, Captain Tyne called out to a rowboat operating as a ferry. "Ahoy, boatman, the two of us are for Gosport Navy Yard. We'll be there for a time. Will you wait for us?"

"Aye, sir, for an hour I will," answered the long-chinned boatman as he reversed his oars, spun his skiff around, and came alongside the dock to hold the boat next to the piling so his passengers could get down into it. Once they were seated, he put his back into the oars, and the skiff fairly flew across the narrow waters.

While they were ferried, Eben and his father talked laughingly about what had happened at this navy yard a few months back. The Yankees had been driven out of it by a very clever ruse. Once war had truly begun and Virginia was declaring secession, the Yankees who held the yard knew that they might be attacked at any time. They were ordered to destroy any war material that might fall into Southern hands. They began to, but before they could finish, Mr. William Mahone, president of the Norfolk and Petersburg Railroad, started sending false messages to the Yankees at the navy yard saying that whole trainloads of Georgia and South Carolina troops were coming in to Norfolk Station. The Yankees didn't know it, but the cars were filled not with men in gray uniforms but with citizens of Norfolk. They cheered and yelled as loudly as possible while the train engineer blew his whistle as the same train chugged back and forth as if it were many trains. How Sam Tyne had regretted not being aboard that day. The Union forces mistakenly believed thousands of Confederates were coming at them.

When the boatman brought his skiff to the edge of the Gosport dock, the Tynes were still chuckling about Mahone's cleverness.

As Eben and his father passed armed guards to enter the yard, Eben told himself he was *here*—at last he was here where he'd always wanted to be. First the *Zephyr,* now this! Right in front of him were the heavy closed doors to the huge dry dock that he knew held the *Merrimack* high and dry inside a great chamber. The secret ship—*his* ship—was in there. How he longed to board her!

Around him, dockworkers were scurrying back and forth among the yard's various buildings as they worked on the many things to be done to ready the *Merrimack* to face the Yankees out in the bay. Some carried long, sharp, whiplike saws; others had big wooden hammers; while yet others used teams of horses to drag treelike timbers to where the ship rested. Eben took all of this activity in at a glance, stopping only a second after entering the dry dock with his father to watch a group of men down at the bottom of the cavernous dock as they worked to re-caulk the hull with tar and oakum.

Then he caught sight of the ship. He had never seen such a vessel! She was huge—nearly 275 feet long, and much wider than the *Zephyr.* But she seemed to him to be only half a ship. From her keel up to her waterline, she was a ship, but everything above the waterline had been cut off. Why, he could even look down into her engine room and see other gangs of men busily setting a great boiler in its place. No, he was wrong. They were taking the boiler out.

He looked on as his father explained. "That's the last of the boilers. There are four of them. That one will have to be rebuilt because it'd been under salt-water for too long after the Yankees sank it."

"Repairing it's going to be a big job, isn't it?" asked Eben. "How long will it take, Pa?"

"Probably it'll be several months before the *Merrimack*'ll be ready to sail. The big problem is getting sheet iron for her. It has to come from rolling mills, and the navy has to wait its turn for iron. The army wants metal, too, for guns and wagon parts, as well as enough to keep the railroads running." Captain Tyne smiled at Eben. "Come on, son, let's go aboard your ship and meet Lieutenant Jones. He's the ship's executive officer. That's the same as first mate, but for now, he's in charge. The *Merrimack* hasn't got any captain yet."

The gangplank to the ship sprang up and down as if it were alive when they walked over it. And, before he knew it, Eben was standing on board the secret ship, the *Merrimack*. He could hardly believe he was really here!

The deck beneath his feet was flat as a griddle cake but very strong. Without being told, he knew that its thick planking and the timbers supporting it had been designed to take the weight of the ship's cannons and to withstand the shock when they were fired, as well as absorb the impact of any hits by Yankee cannon-balls.

Except for the great hole over the engine room, the newly made deck of the *Merrimack* was completed and the workmen were busy making a long scaffolding that rose up from the sides of the deck. This slanted inward at a very sharp angle from the sides of the ship.

As Eben stared in wonder at the great size of its timbers, he didn't notice Catesby ap Jones's approach. Dressed in working clothes, the slightly built young officer came up to Eben's father and smilingly said, "Ah, here you are, Captain Tyne."

Sam Tyne replied, "We were just about to go hunt you up."

"Well, you don't have to do that. Welcome aboard." He paused and looked at Eben. "And this must be your boy, the one who was aboard the *Lucy*."

"Aye, he is. Eben's going to join your ship."

"I'd like that."

Eben then asked the question foremost in his mind. Pointing to the scaffolding, he said, "Please, Sir, what's this?"

Catesby ap Jones walked to an inward-leaning timber and put his hand on it. "These timbers are pitch pine. They're tough. They'll be covered with four inches of fresh white oak and then two layers of two-inch sheet iron." He nodded and went on. "When the iron plating is in place over them, cannonballs and exploding shells will bounce off." As Eben sucked in his breath at the sheer strength and enormity of the

Merrimack, the lieutenant went on talking as if he had given this lecture many times before. "Not only will this ship be armor-plated here on the gun deck, but the plating will go down to three feet under the waterline. That way, we can't be sunk by a low-flying cannonball or by being rammed."

At Eben's gasp of surprise at the thought of so much iron, Jones smiled and added, "Oh, our ship will have a bite, too. She'll carry two rifled cannons and guns at the bow and stern that can pivot. With her big deck guns to port and starboard, she'll whip anything out there."

Here the lieutenant stopped and waved his hand across the expanse of gun deck. "This ship is going to be a match for any Union gun there is! Besides the cannons," the man added, "this ship will have a fifteen-hundred-pound ram made of cast iron. It will be placed just under the waterline on her bow."

A *ram?* Eben knew from his readings in history that the Romans had used rams on their galleys when they fought naval battles hundreds of years before. Rams would crash into the side of another ship, break in its wood sides under the waterline, and then pull away to let the water rush in and sink the enemy vessel. What would this ram do to the Union fleet, he wondered, unconsciously using Catesby ap Jones's word for *Yankee.*

Lieutenant Jones seemed ready to go on talking

about the *Merrimack,* but a tall, gangling man dressed in rust-streaked clothes came up to him, saluted, and said, "Engineer's respects, Sir. Would you come to the engine room right away?"

Returning the salute, Lieutenant Jones excused himself, telling the Tynes, "Look around before you go, and you, my boy, come back to join us after your father leaves. Captain Tyne, I know you're soon leaving the country. I wish you a profitable and safe voyage." Then, turning quickly on his heel, he followed the man belowdecks.

Captain Tyne looked at his pocket watch and said, "All right, we have some time before we're supposed to go back to the skiff. Let's do what the lieutenant says and have a look around."

Eagerly, Eben agreed, and the two of them recrossed the springy gangplank to stand once more on the dock. Eben looked at his ship with even deeper respect now that he knew what type of fighting machine she was to become.

As they walked about, Captain Tyne told Eben more about the navy yard. "When the Yankees ran away," he said, "we gained the best shipyard in the whole country. And we got it without firing a single shot, thanks to William Mahone and our Norfolk patriots. Hundreds of cannon were left behind, plus cannonballs, gunpowder, and ship cordage. Our troops marched in just in time to put out the fires and smother a bomb that was meant to blow up the dry dock. Eben, without that dry dock, there'd be no *Merrimack* to go out and destroy the Yankee blockaders. Let's walk around a bit and then get back to the skiff. I want to spend some time with your mother before I leave tomorrow."

The Tynes walked slowly around the *Merrimack,* examining her from different angles and watching the fevered activity of the dockworkers. Every bit of work seemed to Eben to be centered on the secret ship. Cannon lay in their cradles ready to be shipped aboard. Sheets of rolled iron plate lay in stacks, waiting to be drilled, then bolted to the hull. Men were spinning rope, making boxes that would become the ship cabinets, piling coal, tending forges, and rushing about with sheafs of papers or rolls of the ship's plans in their hands. Here and there stood small groups of engineers hovering over drawings. Eben had never seen so many people hurrying to and fro—under the watchful eyes of guards in Confederate gray—crossing and recrossing each other's paths. Yet it seemed to him that every man here knew what he was up to.

And to think that soon he would be a part of this— part of this great enterprise to give the South victory in the war.

The horsey face of the boatman looked up at them as they climbed into the skiff that would take them across the river. In five minutes, they were back at the Norfolk pier and the boatman was out below the dock circling about for another fare.

On the wharf, Captain Tyne told Eben, "There'll be a skiff waiting for you two days from now. I've arranged it with the *Zephyr's* master. Look for her name painted on it. The skiff will be tied over there." Now he pointed to an iron ring set in the stone of the embankment.

Eben nodded. So, he'd do his own rowing to the *Merrimack*. Good! Feeling proud and looking forward to whatever the future would bring aboard his ship, Eben fell into step with his father as they walked home together. Neither of them spoke of anything but the chores Eben would have to do along with his work in the navy yard.

The following morning was a sad one for everyone Eben cared about. Captain Tyne, Mr. Owens, and Jason boarded the early-morning train headed south. Eben and his mother, who was dry-eyed but nervous, went to the train with them. So did Mrs. Owens and Becky. They all stood somber-faced and silent, watching the two men and Jason, each with his seabag, get on board. As the train pulled out of the brick station, Eben mourned over the many things he had wanted to tell his father but had not had the words to say. Well, his father would understand, but still. . . .

As the train left the station and the figures of the

two men and Jason grew smaller and smaller, Eben was very much aware that now he was the man of the Tyne house, as well as the Owenses' protector.

Gravely, Eben took his mother's arm, called softly to Mrs. Owens and Becky, then summoned a one-horse carriage that was for hire. In silence, the four of them rode back home in unaccustomed style.

That day of farewell went very slowly for Eben. It seemed that his father's leaving had been made sharper by Jason's going, too. Everything was out of kilter now.

Midafternoon, Eben caught himself moping about, wandering between the barn and the house as if he was searching for something. He needed something to keep him busy.

Eben went inside, stuck his head into the parlor, which he was not allowed into unless company called, and said, "Ma, I'm going to rake the pasture and white-wash the chicken coop."

"You do that, Eben" was all Amanda Tyne said, then she sighed.

He stayed busy with chores until it was time for the evening milking. All at once, it came to him that there was no one to milk the Owenses' cow. He went to find her, carrying Jason's bucket and his own stool.

Halfway through the pasture, Becky came running up to him. She watched Eben start the milking. Then she motioned him aside, sat down in his place on his stool, and slowly began milking the Guernsey herself. It was clear to Eben that she'd never done this before, but she sure seemed to have gotten the hang of it fast.

Suddenly, Becky directed a long squirt of milk at Eben, hitting him squarely in the face. What a thing for her to do! This was a game that he and Jason had played while milking together, but he had no idea Becky knew of it. She must have spied on them. Because it was Becky who had done this, Eben didn't flare up. He laughed, then felt the weight of the men's and Jason's leaving drop off him a bit. He was himself again.

The milking done, he and Becky walked back to her house along the same path the boys always used, talking, looking forward to the next milking.

He told her at her back door, "Ma's been acting kind of strange about Pa's leaving and my going to work in the navy yard. She's real quiet and acts kind of mad. What's the matter with her?"

Becky shook her red head. She told him sharply, "Maybe she thinks you shouldn't go . . . that you aren't grown up enough yet for that, Eben, even if you were aboard the *Lucy* and did well there. That was awfully dangerous for you and it scared us."

Saying that, Becky Owens ran inside with the milk, leaving Eben to tousle his hair while wondering at her words.

CHAPTER SIX

THE NEW DOCKHAND

Heading the following morning for the *Zephyr*'s neat white-painted skiff to row himself across the river, Eben felt proud. This would be his first day as a sailor in the Confederate Navy and as a crew member of the *Merrimack*. What Virginia-born boy could ask for anything better?

His route took him along a narrow path of tallish shrubbery growing behind a row of picket fences. As Eben came to the end of the path, Jamie Sloat stepped out to bar his way. There he stood, fists balled on his hips, glaring.

Eben let out a sigh. He'd been half expecting this, and now it was here!

Jamie shouted at Eben, whose own anger was mounting to match the other boy's. "I know where you're off to, bat ears. You're going over to the navy yard, ain't you? Lordy, but you think you're a big fish now that you're working with sailors. You're getting out of going to school like Jason did, but the rest of us got to keep going there. You can fight me right now or fight me later. I want to fight right now."

Eben was exasperated. Fight? Sure, he'd fight Jamie Sloat when he had the time, but right now he didn't. They expected him at his ship. Well, he could outrun Jamie anytime he wanted to, and now was one of those times.

Digging his toes in for speed, Eben raced toward the unsuspecting Jamie, hit him hard, bowling him over, leaped his body, and sprinted for the docks and the skiff.

A quick glance behind him showed Jamie floundering on the ground, shouting his rage. As the boy got clumsily to his feet, a tall woman came through a gate set in the shrubbery to swat him about the head and shoulders with a broom. Her lambasting made Jamie run in the opposite direction and made Eben laugh.

However, in his exultant moment something festered—the memory of Jamie on the ground rolling about. Had he been *crying?* His face certainly had been twisted as if he might have been. Jamie had been humiliated by him and by the woman, too. All at once,

Eben felt sorry for Jamie Sloat, who had to listen to Becky brag about him and Jason being heroes for the South. Nobody could brag like Becky when she got going at it. The Tyne and Owens families were richer than the Sloats were by far.

Suddenly, Eben realized why Jamie disliked him—Jamie was jealous! That was it. Jealous of him, Eben! Jamie would love to go over to the secret ship, too, instead of sitting day after day among pupils younger than he was.

Eben rowed to the yard that morning thinking of Jamie, but as he arrived, he thought of his ship. After tying the skiff to the ringbolt, he passed the guards and walked over the springy gangplank to the ironclad. Once on board, he found Catesby ap Jones. Saluting as he had seen the rust-covered man do the other day, Eben reported himself ready for duty. His salute was politely returned.

The officer asked Eben whether his father had left on his voyage, and when he heard Captain Tyne had gone, he said, "Now, boy, what am I to do with you right now before we sail? I think I want you to report to Mr. Brooke for duty. He's our expert on armament. You will find him in the first shed beyond that big stack of cannonballs." Lieutenant Jones pointed to one side of the ship. "Go there now. Tell him you're part of this ship's crew. He'll find work for you to do. I'll see you from time to time. Welcome aboard, lad."

"Aye, Sir, glad to be aboard!" Eben replied properly as he saluted once more. Then he turned and left the executive officer.

As the boy entered the shed, he saw that there were nearly thirty men hard at work inside. A blue haze of smoke sifted out its open ends. The smells of burning charcoal in the forges, oil and metal shavings from the lathes, plus the steam of red-hot rods being plunged into barrels of water to temper the steel assaulted Eben's nose. Hammers clanged on anvils. Metal clattered as pieces were pulled from piles. Men called out as their sledges pounded the hot cast pig iron into supple wrought iron.

At first glance, it appeared to Eben like the hell that the minister warned against in church—stenches, flames, and confusion. He soon saw, though, that the men were working in teams. There wasn't any wasted motion. Every job was done as well and as quickly as possible.

One officer stood out from the others as he went quietly from one group to another. Here he pointed out something. There he spoke briefly with whoever seemed to be the leader of that group. Yes, that tall, thin, long-bearded man had to be Mr. Brooke.

Eben reported to him the minute the officer was through talking to a worker. Mr. Brooke shook the boy's hand, enveloping it in the sinewy one of a blacksmith as he welcomed him to the Armament Department, as he called the shack.

Eben was relieved and happy to see that the man already knew about him and that he had been expecting him. When Catesby ap Jones seemed at a loss about Eben's presence, the boy had been worried, but now he knew the lieutenant had only been joking with him.

Mr. Brooke said, "So, you'd be the lad who set the torpedoes in the bay and put an end to the Yankee gunboat? Well, come on, I'll show you about. I'm not so busy now. The quicker you know what we're doing in here, the quicker you can be of use to us. The only way to help here is to know what you're about. Never fear to ask anybody a question. That way, we work faster and have fewer accidents."

"Aye, Sir, I understand." This wasn't too different from school, where he asked questions, too.

"Good. I have just the job for you. It's an important one. It is going to take a lot of attention and care, though, and mostly you'll be working by yourself. But first, you have a general look-see, huh?"

Guiding Eben, Mr. Brooke walked him through the big shed, stopping to show him how the wrought iron was made, explaining that its toughness would withstand the pressures of firing the cannon, whereas cast metal would explode from the stress and most likely kill the gun crew when the cannon blew up. They went by the gleaming coals in the forge, where cannon barrels were heating, then would be pounded, reheated, and repounded again to toughen the metal.

"We have to do all this," Brooke explained, "to make sure the guns serve us well. The cannon you see right now were left behind by the Yankees when the yard was evacuated. We aren't sure they were in top condition then. What we're doing now is hammering them to restrengthen the metal. Then we know they'll do the job! All of them will be test-fired before being taken on board our ship for service. Over there," he continued, pointing to the rear of the shed, "are the pivot guns. Let's go take a look at them."

Walking to the two guns, Brooke explained how they had been designed to work on a swivel. They could point left or right or up or down without having to be moved by men pulling them with tackles.

Finally, the *Merrimack*'s armaments officer walked to a pair of slim, long cannon that rested on a sturdy bench. Looking down the length of one of them, Eben guessed they would become the rifled cannon that Lieutenant Catesby ap Jones had spoken of. He suddenly wondered whether these cannon had been saved until the last for some purpose.

He was right. Mr. Brooke told him, "Eben, these guns will be your friends for the next month or so. They will be set in the bow of our ship. Your job will be special, and every move you make must be exact.

Don't hurry your work. When you're finished, these two cannon will be the straightest, hardest-shooting guns we have. I'll explain all of this to you tomorrow. Bring old clothes to work and always be sure to wear shoes. The work will be dirty, and metal filings are sharp."

Now Mr. Brooke looked hard at Eben out of serious, dark eyes. "What I want you to be right now is a dockworker. The best thing for you to do today is to learn the navy yard. What I mean is, walk all over it. But stay out of the way while you do. See everything you can and fix it in your memory. Remember where supplies are kept." He gazed at Eben and patted his shoulder. "If I send you out tomorrow morning for half-inch cable, I want you to know where to pick it up. So today you learn the yard. Tomorrow you start work on these guns. Any questions? None, good! Well, until tomorrow then!"

Any questions? Eben looked at the two cannon on the bench and bit his lower lip. Why, for one thing, what was *he* to do with *them?* This wasn't like school, where things are explained right away. Well, he'd find out tomorrow.

Eben walked about scrutinizing work and workers with deep interest. There was so much to see, so much to bear in mind. Just looking around was hard work. He would have to know a lot about this by tomorrow.

But where to start? Mr. Brooke was working with guns. Therefore, the things he would be most interested in would have to do with metal. That made sense. That would be foundry work. He would find the foundry next.

Eben located the foundry. It was at the back of the shipyard, next to where the railroad line ended. Here he watched the blacksmiths work iron into marine fittings for his ship, pouring molten iron from the coke oven into sand molds. The odor of hot cooking metal was everywhere. He had thought the smell of the gun shop unpleasant, but it didn't compare with this. Enough was enough, and he soon beat a hasty retreat to inspect the boiler shop and look at the four big boilers of the *Merrimack*'s two engines.

Everywhere, he saw the same sense of purpose, the same rushing to get things done. An enormous amount of work was being performed as fast as possible in a small area—so much so that it seemed on first look like complete confusion.

With all the noise and all the people here, Eben wondered how this could ever be kept a secret from the Yankees. Until his father had brought him here, all he'd ever heard was that there was a secret ship in Gosport Navy Yard. But what did the Yankees know?

By midafternoon, Eben Tyne had made three tours of the shipyard. Mr. Brooke wasn't going to catch him napping tomorrow! "If he wants rope," Eben told himself out loud, "I know where to get it. If it's lumber, all he has to do is tell me the size. Fetch nuts, bolts, screws, take messages to other shops—I'll be ready for him."

Late in the day, Eben took the same route homeward, wondering as he walked whether Jamie would waylay him once again. As he went past the fences and shrubbery, though, nothing happened except that a brown dog barked at him from behind a gate. Eben thought of Jamie as he went along and found himself truly sorry for him. Life wasn't exciting for Jamie. Nobody called him a hero. No teachers at the little school he, Jason, and Becky attended had ever taken to any of the Sloats. They had taken to Eben and the Owenses. Always having somebody down on a person could make a body mean-natured, couldn't it?

Eben hoped he wouldn't have to fight Jamie anymore. It wasn't that he couldn't lick him right and proper; it was that it was getting to be a childish thing to do. After having been aboard the *Lucy* in that scrap and now working on the *Merrimack,* rolling around in the dirt punching Jamie seemed a pretty useless thing to do.

Once past the shrubbery path, Eben put Jamie out of his mind and focused on the mysterious thing he was to do.

A very excited Eben Tyne rowed across the river the next morning and expectantly walked with Mr. Brooke to the two cannon he had seen last. He'd left so early, his mother had put out a cold breakfast for him the night before and had not come down to bid him good-bye. She hadn't said a word when he told her he would be wearing his oldest clothes and stoutest shoes.

Eben stood beside Mr. Brooke looking at the guns. Now he would find out what he was to do. Eagerly, he looked on, but his heart fell in disappointment when the officer brought out a long hickory-wood pole from the corner of the shed. Would he be working only with a wooden pole? The pole was as long as the cannon barrel and had an odd-looking rakelike fixture made of steel on one end. Eben watched Mr. Brooke shove the pole far down in the barrel of the cannon so the metal rake was nearly at its far end. Then the officer pulled it out. As he did, Eben saw the hickory shaft rotate in his hands. The rake was a cutting tool, Brooke explained swiftly. Eben's job would be to use it to cut spiral grooves in the smooth barrels of the cannons.

Pleased that Eben understood without a lengthy explanation, Mr. Brooke showed him exactly how he was to use the rake. Then he said, "The grooves you'll cut in these barrels will make the shell spin when the gun is fired. It'll be like throwing a rock or a ball overhand so it flies true. These cannon are for long-distance firing; they will be able to hit their mark precisely from far away, lad."

Brooke cautioned the boy. "Take your time now. It'll take several days to cut a rifling groove of the proper depth. When you've finished the first one, start the other. The work's slow. You're going to think you don't make any headway from hour to hour, because you can't see the results in the metal barrel. But with each one of your thrusts and withdrawals, tiny slivers of metal will be carved out. Stay with it, son. It's not muscle work, it's craftsmanship; and that means more. I've been told you take pride in what you do. This is what all of us who work on the *Merrimack* feel. She's to be our handiwork—our present to the Confederacy."

The officer stood by to watch Eben make the first cut, then showed him how to oil and adjust the cutting blade. He looked on as the boy set to work and he inspected the first dozen strokes. Then he patted Eben on the shoulder and hurried back to join men working on another cannon.

Day after day, week after week, for a full five weeks, Eben laboriously cut the rifling in the pair of cannon. Each morning he rowed to the navy yard, and each night he rowed home to do his family's chores, as well as most of the Owenses'. His mother seemed to have grown more quiet, and she didn't talk to him much about his work. Eben felt that was hardly surprising since it was secret. It was also very dull. It took much sighing and all of his patience to keep at it day after day.

He could hardly believe it when he pulled the rod from the last groove on the second cannon and measured its depth of cut. It was exact—just like the first gun. Eben didn't waste any time running to find Mr. Brooke and tell him.

The businesslike officer smiled down at him. He said, "Well, lad, that means the guns are ready for their test firing. We'll fire these and the other guns tomorrow. Would you like to watch?"

Would I, thought Eben excitedly.

He looked on in pride as his guns were mounted. They meant much to him—they were *his* gift to the Confederacy. Long, sleek, and dangerous-looking, their black mouths already defied any enemy. Tomorrow they would be tested to prove they were strong enough and to adjust their gunsights so that they would hit their targets. How would they do?

Eben walked back to his skiff that night, lost in the prospect of the next day's firing, his first job in the navy yard finished. As he went past the *Merrimack,* it came to him that he had been so busy cutting the rifling that he hadn't kept track of the progress of his ship in her refitting. There she lay, deep in her cavern of dry dock. Her underhull was completed. Her big propeller gleamed with its recent buffings. The bare scaffolding that went up from her gun deck had been sheathed with heavy oak planks and sheets of plate iron. Yes, sir, thought Eben, she was getting ready to fight—to attack the blockaders!

He felt a shiver go through him as he thought of the ten guns she would carry. There would be more than a hundred ship's cannons out there ready for her. However, the *Merrimack* was iron-plated, just like a knight in armor, and her sides were slanted like a shield. The Yankee shots could bounce off her like arrows had bounced off Ivanhoe's armor. That's what they were all counting on—Lieutenant Catesby ap Jones, Mr. Brooke, and Eben Tyne.

The workers of the navy yard had been busy long before daylight to ready the targets and the guns for the testing. As Eben walked up to the armament shed, he saw that all the cannons had been rolled out of the building.

Each was to be fired against a wooden wall the thickness of an ordinary ship's hull. Eben took powder to the first big gun and watched its loading. There came a thunderous roar and spurt of flame as it was fired. Its cannonball went through the wall cleanly. The cannon's terrible sound made Eben shudder. No, cannons were never to be loved—only deeply respected as horrible instruments of war.

Now he was ordered to fetch powder for the pivot guns. He heard their loud *snap* and took note of how they blasted log targets apart. The logs were meant to represent the rigging and masts of enemy sailing ships.

His own rifled cannons came last. This time, plate iron was set before the same wooden wall into which the first cannons had fired. His guns were to be sharp shooters, not blasters.

Before they were fired, Mr. Brooke told the gun crews, "We have heard rumors from spies that there may be an ironclad being built by the Yankees, too. Secrets like this are hard to keep. These guns will be needed against her if the rumors are true."

Eben took gunpowder over once more and saw his cannon loaded with it. Their sights were lined up on chalk marks Mr. Brooke drew on the iron. When they were ready, the officer nodded to the gunner.

Then a surprising thing happened. The tall brown-haired gunner named Kendrick handed the match to Eben instead of putting it to the touchhole himself.

Eben stared at the flying fish tattooed on the sun-browned hand that held the match. He, Eben Tyne, was to be given the honor of firing his cannon for the first time, and by a sailor who had been to Hong Kong.

Was it because of what he'd done on the *Lucy,* or because he'd rifled this very gun?

Trembling, holding his breath, Eben took the match and put it to the touchhole, the little hole bored into the top of the cannon barrel and filled with fine powder. The match's small blaze would travel down the gun barrel to the rough black powder he had carried to it and would make the cannon fire.

It did! His cannon's report was a sharp, whiplike crack of angry defiance. It was high-pitched, not at all like the sullen low roar of the bigger guns, the Dahlgrens. Its ball punched a neat round hole through the iron plate, right on target. Hurray! Eben knew he had done his job well!

When the testing was finished, Mr. Brooke ordered the same men to clean and oil all the guns. After that, spare cannons that would be used to train the crews were brought out. These guns would be filled with sawdust bags, not gunpowder.

When all was made ready, the gunner who had handed Eben the match called a large number of men standing nearby him and said, "I'm to be gun captain of this rifled cannon. Other gun captains will be named later." His sharp hazel eyes swept the group of men, then stopped at Eben. He grinned and said, "Tyne, you're to be powdermonkey for this gun. You fired it first and you rifled it, so I choose you first."

Powderboy! Powdermonkey to one of his own guns! Eben's breath caught in this throat.

The master gunner told him, "Powderboy Tyne, lay off to port, just behind this gun. Wait there."

Lowering his voice to make it sound deeper and older, Eben answered, "Aye, Sir." Then, hands in his pockets, walking with a roll like the deep-sea men, he sauntered over to the spot where the gunner had pointed. Eben guessed he was really in the navy now.

CHAPTER SEVEN

POWDERMONKEY!

Now wasn't this something to be proud of! It might be dangerous, but wasn't everything dangerous aboard a ship of war?

In a glow of pride, Eben listened to his gun captain say, "I'd be Tom Kendrick. I was a gunner in the old navy. Now all men here who have served cannons in the past, fall out to the starboard. The rest of you, stand fast."

Eben looked on as nearly thirty men moved off to the right. Then Kendrick sang out, "All men from the U.S.S. *Essex,* pay off to port." At this order, six who had formerly served on that frigate moved slightly to the left of their group. Swiftly, the gun captain singled out crew members who had served on other navy ships of war, forming them into other groups. Within minutes, there were eight groups of shipmates, but not one man among them had ever served as a gun captain on any ship.

"Right now," Kendrick said, "the most experienced man in each group will be acting gun captain. We'll choose them as we train." He spoke with the ease of one used to command. "The rest of you be ready to make up part of the gun crews we need. We want to have thirteen fully trained crews when we're done. You know the reason why, though we only have ten guns."

Silence followed this remark. Everyone knew there would be casualties. Kendrick put their fears somewhat to rest by saying, "No, we won't lose a full gun crew to the enemy. I promise you that, if you train to the best of your ability the way I'll teach you. We'll start the drills tomorrow two hours after sunup. First, there'll be a walk-through drill. Then we're going to train on the guns aboard our ship. Teamwork, and a lot of it, will turn you into first-rate gun crews."

Then the master gunner began calling out names for his gun crew. "James," he shouted out first, and a big blond man stepped forward. Kendrick told him, "I remember you from our time together on the *Savannah*." The next men called were also large and very muscular, as befit men who had to lift cannonballs to the cannon's mouth.

Kendrick went on calling names until he got to the very last one. "Jack Rawlins," he shouted out, "you'll be handling the sponge to clean out the cannon once it's been fired and will act as alternate shot man if some man is disabled."

"Aye, Sir! It'll be like the old days, eh?" was the soft-voiced reply of a smallish man who came out of the group moving with a natural, measured grace. His clean-shaven face was brown, his hair shining and curly auburn. His features were sharp, and his eyes so light a blue that they looked transparent. At once, Eben liked the looks of him.

That evening, Eben and his mother spoke for a time after supper. He hadn't talked much to her lately because he'd come home from the shipyard weary. He felt guilty for neglecting her, so he was glad when she asked him to sit with her awhile at the table.

Of course, Amanda Tyne heard the booming when the test cannons had been fired. Everybody in and around Norfolk had. She told Eben, "I trust that dreadful noise won't go on every day from now on. I'd like to forget the war now and then."

"No, Ma, they're done testing. The gunners found out what they need to know by now. Ma, I fired my cannon myself today—the one I worked on! The gunner gave me the match and let me fire it. I guess that means I'm really in the navy now, huh?"

"You, a boy, fired a cannon! They let you do that?" Mrs. Tyne's eyes grew wide with shock.

"It wouldn't blow up on me. It wasn't dangerous."

"*Not dangerous?* All firearms are dangerous, Eben. So you are working in a gun crew now?"

"Looks that way."

"Have you signed any papers yet, son?"

"No."

Amanda Tyne nodded her head, got up, took the lamp, and told him, "I have to see to the chickens now. Becky told me she spotted a fox around the hen house."

"I'll do that for you, Ma."

"All right. Thank you, Eben."

By the time Eben came back from his inspection, having seen nothing more than the hens asleep at roost, his mother had gone upstairs. He stood a long moment, disappointed. He'd wanted to tell her about Gunner Kendrick and Jack Rawlins and Mr. Brooke and Lieutenant Jones. She ought to be interested in the men he worked with, but she hadn't asked him one word about them. Pa would have wanted to know everything. He wondered why she didn't.

Kendrick's walk-through drill the next morning was a repeat of the firing of the day before. Now, however, the gunner talked about the duties of each man, explaining the need for teamwork and for taking safety measures to keep from any accidental firing of the great guns. The drill was soon over, and everyone, except for Eben, knew what he was to do.

At a call from the ship, Kendrick formed his crews and marched them to the side of the *Merrimack,* where cannons waited to be hoisted aboard. For the next three hours, the gun crews worked to install the guns in their battle positions. Then loading rammers, chamber sponges, unloading screws on long poles, and water buckets were placed where they would be easily accessible. From gun to gun, the locations of these tools did not vary a single inch!

Every item was closely inspected by the master gunner. When he was satisifed, Kendrick called the gun crews together and told them, "You can see how everything is laid out. Look at each gun. Remember where it is. Every time these tools"—he pointed to each in turn—"are placed, they are to be set in the *exact same location*—not even six inches away." Stopping to search the faces of the listeners, he went on in a serious voice. "Your life and those of your shipmates will depend on this. When we fight from the gun deck, you will see why. The noise from the guns will hit you like thunder. Your eyesight will dim from the powder smoke. Most of you are going to be halfsick with fear. Expect to be! I know I will be."

His voice turned harsh and his face hardened as if he recalled some past action in his own career. Eben saw how he gazed directly at Jack Rawlins. Aye, they had seen battle together.

Kendrick now went on normally. "What I mean is that you have to know where everything is. You have to be able to grab it and use it even if you can't see it!"

For nearly an hour, the gun crews practiced moving to and from their equipment. First, they counted their steps, and then walked blindfolded until each man could place his hand on the sponge, rammer, powder charge, and cannonball as soon as each was called for.

Satisfied at last, Kendrick called the crew together again. As he spoke to them, Jack Rawlins, at a wink from the gunner, moved along the line of cannons rearranging the positions and locations of the various tools.

When he was finished, Kendrick ordered, "Back to your guns, men. Stand ready, and on my command, go to your posts."

Confidently, the crews returned to their guns. However, when they were ordered "Load your pieces!" at once there was confusion. Hands grabbed automatically for the rammer or sponge or bucket, but could not find it there. The earlier precision was gone. Tempers flared.

Blowing a high-pitched note on his boatswain's

pipe, Gunner Kendrick called the men together again and said, "That's a little taste of what you'll be getting if you make mistakes. Every tool must be in its place at all times."

Now he ordered, "You're at liberty now. You have forty minutes to look over your ship. Stay out of the way of work crews, but get a good look at everything. On a ship in battle, men do jobs as they are needed."

As the crews spread out to acquaint themselves with the *Merrimack,* Eben held back, measuring the length of the gun deck with his eyes. Like long black bottles, the rifle cannons sat port and starboard. He wondered what it would be like to fire his in battle. Well, he knew something about fighting, didn't he? He'd been aboard the *Lucy* and been fired on. What would it be like to fire back?

Suddenly, he became aware of Seaman Rawlins at his side. The man said, "This is a different world now, isn't it? Brother fights brother, and each one for the cause he thinks is the right one. Civil war's the worst kind of war. This won't be like shooting at pirates out of Tunis or the big slave ships sailing the Caribbean or . . ." He drifted off now after the members of his gun crew, leaving his sentence unfinished.

Thinking about the truth of Rawlins's words, Eben turned his attention to his ship. It wouldn't be long before she would be ready, he told himself. She might even be ready by Christmastime. The arrival of Christmas meant even more work for him. He would have to get busy at night and carve more wooden ducks to sell as decoys in Norfolk. That was how he earned money to buy presents for his family and the Owenses. Maybe with fair winds, his father and Jason would be home by then—but he doubted that.

Pondering duck decoys, he heard the loud call "Form up!" Running to join his group, Eben was stopped by Jack Rawlins, who grabbed him by the arm and hissed, "Never run aboard a ship. Walk rapidly, but don't you ever run!"

Embarrassed at forgetting something he had already been told, Eben walked rapidly to join his crew.

Kendrick again ordered his men together, having them form a circle around one of the cannon. Three cannonballs were laid out in a line on either side of the muzzle of the gun. The novice crews would now learn how to load their cannons.

At Kendrick's instruction, the powderman of the first crew brought the sawdust-filled bags to the muzzle of the gun and pushed them into its bore. That crew's number-one shot man rammed the sawdust home with the long rammer and removed the rammer so the number-two shot man could put the big ball into the muzzle, step back, and help number one ram it home to sit snugly against the powder bags.

The powderman now went back to the powder box behind the gun as the gun captain went through the motions of priming the piece. Then he signaled the tacklemen as they pulled the cannon forward to poke its muzzle out between the two poles representing the ship's side.

The master gunner now showed the gun crew how to change the direction in which the cannon was pointing, as well as to elevate the muzzle. Then he said, "Now I touch the match, and the gun will fire—or would fire if I was using real gunpowder, not sawdust."

After the gun crew withdrew the charge and sawdust-filled powder bag, and moved the gun back to its original position, Rawlins took the long-handled sponge, wet it in the water bucket, and swiftly sponged out the bore of the gun. While he did this, the gunner explained that this had to be done after each shot. Otherwise, any smoldering pieces of powder bag still inside the gun could set off the new powder being rammed into it.

Finally, Kendrick turned sharply to Eben. "Powderboy Tyne, your job in a battle is to see that the gunpowder box is kept filled. You'll go belowdecks where the powder is stored in the powder magazine and bring it up to us. Bring just enough to keep us shooting—no more than that. The box over there will hold eleven full bags. You are also to see to it that the sponge bucket is kept filled with water."

"Aye, aye, Sir," said Eben.

"All right, you men. Crew by crew, we're going to

practice loading, aiming, shooting, and reloading. I want you to be able to do this with your eyes closed. That way we can work the guns shorthanded if any member of the gun crew is wounded in a fight. Just maybe, once you can do this without stopping to think about it, you will be able to call yourselves cannoneers. Now, to the drill again."

Day after day, the merciless drilling continued. There was no letup in the training. In those long weeks from late September through October and November, Eben managed to carve four decoy ducks at home, for which he received two dollars in Norfolk. With that money and his very small wages from the *Merrimack,* he bought combs and handkerchiefs for his mother and the Owens women.

Christmas was quietly sad that year with Captain Tyne and Jason and his father away. During previous overseas voyages, there had been messages, because friendly ships would heave to in mid-ocean to catch up on the news of the world and to pass on letters, but this holiday season there were no letters from either Eben's father or the Owens men. Eben could see how dearly they were missed at this festive time of the year.

The two families shared their holiday. Amanda Tyne and Mrs. Owens and Becky gave Eben handknitted mittens, a jacket, a scarf, and a cap to wear on the cold gun deck of his ship. They all went to church together. The congregation sang the usual holiday carols, but there weren't any tenor and baritone voices to sound the deeper notes. Most of the men were gone. It was women and children, boys and old men who did the singing. Looking around the church, Eben spotted Jamie Sloat at the back, glowering at him. Eben looked away. Today wasn't any day to have trouble with him.

The Owenses had their Christmas dinner at the Tyne home. Amanda Tyne carved the goose because nobody trusted Eben with that delicate work. She didn't do it too well, he noticed—not as well as his pa did each year—but at least she did it fast enough so the meat came warm to their plates. Eben saw the tears she wiped away as she brought the plum pudding to the table. That had always been a special moment for them in past years because that's when Sam Tyne had always called out in his deepest voice, "God bless us, everyone!"—words from the little book by Charles Dickens that was read aloud each year to Eben when he was small. He and Becky and their mothers would have to keep on waiting and hoping and stay strong in their faith that everything would work out all right in the new year.

As the gun crews assembled to run through their drills yet again on the sleet- and rain-filled morning of January 23, Gunner Kendrick surprised his men by summoning Mr. Brooke.

As the officer watched attentively, the master gunner called out, "Column of gun crews. Left face. Quick step. Halt!"

To a man, the crew knew their days of make-believe drills were over; now they were to ready the gun as if for real battle. They went to their stations, each crew to its own gun, and waited.

At the sound of the order from Kendrick, men jumped to their work, and in very short order the cannon were loaded and in position.

Now at last, Eben's job became the real thing. He saw the great responsibility to his gun crew that was his alone. As he had done in the countless drills before this, Eben left his six-inch gun, hurried down the gun deck to the companionway, went down the ladder to the mid-deck, and then down once more to the lower deck below the waterline. Here the deck beams were so low that even he, small as he was, had to stoop as he ducked under the great wooden knees that supported the decking over his head—this was why powdermonkeys were always boys, never grown men. As he made his way to a cubbyhole near the bow, he moved rapidly at a walk. He had to warn himself not to run. Would he remember to walk when the fighting started? Cold fear gripped him for a moment: Would it be like it had been aboard the *Lucy?* No, of course not; this was an ironclad.

There was no direct light near the powder locker, only the glimmer of two hooded whale-oil lamps set nearly twenty feet from the powder. Eben's work would be done by feel more than by sight. It had to be that way. The powder must be protected from fire. For fear of accidentally making a spark and causing a fire, he wasn't allowed to carry his barlow knife. He also had to move barefooted, as any spark from his leather-soled shoes could spell disaster for his ship.

Lined up beside the other powderboys, Eben quickly took his turn at grabbing a twelve-pound powder charge for his gun, cradling it to his chest, and getting a second one for his other arm. He walked swiftly back to his cannon, placed the charges in the ready locker, and dived belowdecks again to the magazine.

Midway through that first drill with live ammunition, the first accident took place. The nervous powderboy of the center Dahlgren on the port side tripped and fell down the companionway as he hastened to the lower deck. As he tried to save himself from his headlong fall, he broke his arm. The ship's doctor splinted it where he lay on the deck.

Gunner Kendrick was not pleased to be shorthanded. He didn't have extra powderboys, and now he had to find one! "Tyne," he called to Eben, "I need another boy like you. Can you get me one? Have him here for duty by the second hour tomorrow. You can train him the first hour. Then I'll turn him over to the gun crew as a replacement. Any questions?"

"No, Sir. A new powdermonkey to you by the second hour tomorrow."

"On your way, then—smartly now. Dismissed."

"Aye, Sir."

As Eben rowed across the Elizabeth, bundled up against the winter chill in all his Christmas finery, he wondered to himself where he would find a replacement powderboy at such short notice. Jason would have been perfect. Oh, well, that was a wasted thought! There just had to be somebody else—somebody somewhere, not too tall but strong.

Yep, there was somebody! The idea galled him, but there was someone! Eben spun the skiff in the river and made for the dock closest to the *Sarah*. The closer he came to it, the more pleased he was with his idea. It could be just harebrained enough to work.

Tying the skiff's line to the dock, Eben jumped out and ran, enjoying the sprinting forbidden to him on board the *Merrimack*. He ran to the cluster of older buildings at the far end of Norfolk's Taylor Street. Even the cobblestones here were loose and in need of repair. This was a poor section of the city.

Eben stopped in front of one of the old houses, rapped boldly on its scarred, unpainted front door, and stood back waiting for it to open.

A middle-aged woman with dark hair answered his knock. She swayed a bit as she looked at him out of watery eyes and asked, "What ya want, boy?"

Remembering Jamie's glowering at him in church, Eben asked Mrs. Sloat, "Is Jamie home?" Would Jamie be willing to do his bit for the South or not? Maybe somebody else ought to ask him. Somebody he liked.

"Jamie? What you want with him?" she asked, but she called out hoarsely, "Jamie, you git out here now!" Then she turned and disappeared inside without another word.

All at once, a ruckus of loud voices arose from within. Everybody seemed to be yelling at once. This home, Eben thought, is like a hornet's nest. He was about to leave when Jamie stepped out the door and closed it.

There was both curiosity and surliness on the boy's broad face as he stood in front of Eben and about a foot higher than he was on the steps. Jamie came down to face him. Eben returned his stare, then sat down on the bottom step and looked as calmly as he could out onto Taylor Street. Jamie sat down, too. His clenched fists making lumps in his pockets, he waited for Eben to speak.

Eben said, "Pretty cold out here, ain't it?"

After a time, Jamie answered, "Yeah, but it's quiet; not like back in there with all my brothers and sisters. They're always up to some devilment."

"Yeah," Eben replied; then came the words: "I need your help. I didn't come here to fight with you."

"You're sure you didn't come here to scrap, huh?"

"Honest. I—no, *we* need your help."

"Who'd 'we' be?"

Eben drew a deep breath. "The South! Jamie, I couldn't tell you before, but I'm a powderboy on the secret ship they're building over at Gosport Navy Yard. She's the *Merrimack*. Do you know much about her?"

"I guess I know as much as most folks do. So that's what you been up to instead of going to school."

Eben went on. "She's going out to fight the Yankee blockaders pretty soon. We had an accident today. One of the powderboys got careless and was hurt. Now we're one good hand short. The secret ship needs a powderboy." Eben stopped to allow his classmate time to think this over.

Jamie took a walnut from his pocket, studied it, cracked it, ate the meat, and threw the hull into the street. He said nothing.

"Jamie," Eben started again, "I've been sent to find the hand we need to become a member of the gun crew. We need somebody we can depend on . . . and we've got to have him come aboard *tomorrow*."

"Tomorrow?"

"I came to you, Jamie, 'cause I just thought you might know somebody who'd fit the bill." Here Eben stopped again and looked back into the other boy's face. "Of course, I could be wrong, and maybe you don't." Eben knew the only way to overcome Jamie's stubbornness was by being more clever than he.

The second nut came out of Jamie's pocket. With

a bit of rummaging, a third joined it. Wordlessly, Jamie passed one to Eben. The boys cracked them, munching the sweet meat in silence.

Finally, Jamie asked again, "Tomorrow, huh?"

"Yeah, tomorrow morning. If you know anybody like that, you tell him to be at the dock across from the yard right early, by the skiff from the *Zephyr* that's tied there. I'll row him over. Thanks for the nut. Reckon I'd better go home now. I got chores to do for my ma and for Jason's folks, too."

"Yeah, Eben."

Eben walked nearly a full block up Taylor Street before he bent down to pick up a loose stone. As he did, he sneaked a backward glance under his arm. Jamie hadn't moved from the step. He was smiling as he started to crack another walnut, though. What did his smile mean? Eben tossed the rock away and walked off. He would find out tomorrow!

· CHAPTER EIGHT ·

SPIES AND TROUBLE AT HOME

The next morning, though concerned that he may not have gotten Gunner Kendrick a powderboy, Eben woke up to some small joy at least. A soft blanket of snow covered everything outside. After he and Becky milked their cows, they had a fierce snowball fight; but all too soon that fun was over and Eben had to be on his way back to his ship.

His quick temper flashed as he saw that there was nobody on the dock where he tied his skiff. Its snow-covered length was deserted. All that clever talk had gone for nothing. Jamie hadn't come. Eben would have to report his failure to the gun captain just as the man had begun to place his trust in him. Darn that Jamie, and darn himself for believing in him.

Eben went to the dock's edge and looked down to where the skiff bobbed in the ebb tide. Nobody was down in it. Well, he'd best get on with this bad business and face Kendrick's possible anger and disappointment.

As Eben started for the ladder to the skiff, he saw a support piling on the dock move. It split in two, and one brown half walked toward him. It was Jamie, in old brown trousers and a jacket, like always. He had come after all!

Coming up to Eben, Jamie tossed a small sack of belongings onto the floorboards of the skiff, gave him a nod, and climbed down. "Ma don't care if I leave. It's one less of us to feed. I'll see she gets some of my pay money. It's been hard since Pa ran out on us. Let me row, Eben. I can do it real well."

Matching Jamie's nonchalant manner, Eben handed over the oars without a smile, though inwardly happy to see Jamie. Jamie took the oars. Surprisingly, he was a dandy oarsman, Eben soon learned. Well, the *Merrimack* had got herself a new powdermonkey!

Jamie Sloat took to his duties like a young colt to a sweet clover patch. As he taught Jamie his duties, it occurred to Eben that this may have been the first time the other boy had ever been given some responsibility and respect, and the chance to do something without being bullied or teased. He seemed a different boy now. He was mighty quick to catch on to things. Within hours, he was helping other boys in their drill as they scurried, carrying charges for their guns. Eben knew he had done the right thing in going to him.

As he was getting ready to row home to Norfolk later that day, Eben sought out Jamie to take him with him. "I'll be shoving off in a minute, Jamie. Are you ready?" Eben said.

Jamie shook his shaggy head. "No, I'm going to stay aboard. Mr. Brooke said I can sleep in the powder magazine. He told me to sling myself a hammock between the guns of the gun deck, but I can sleep on top of the powder bags just as well. It'll be better for me that way, Eben. I told ya, Ma don't want me back. I reckon I can be a guard down there. They need me just like you said. Thanks, Eben. See ya tomorrow."

"See you tomorrow" was Eben's answer. He couldn't think of anything more to say to the chunky boy standing in front of him. He realized they finally understood each other. There would be no more fighting between them from now on. Good! Fighting Jamie would be a waste of time and energy, and it sure could put up the gunners' backs against both of them.

The following day was filled with surprises. As Amanda Tyne sat darning one of her son's socks at the breakfast table, she looked at him as he ate and asked sharply, "When will your ship be sailing, Eben?"

Taken aback by her question, one she had never asked him before, he told her, "I don't know, Ma. And even if I did, I couldn't tell you. But nobody tells us powdermonkeys anything."

Mrs. Tyne put down her mending. "Eben, I told you this before, and I'll tell you again. I wish you weren't a powderboy."

"But, Ma, that's the only thing boys my age can do on a warship."

"I wish your ship was not a warship."

"Oh, Ma. She's a wonderful ship."

"Eben, I've spoken my piece for now," said his mother, and jabbed the needle into the sock as she went back to darning.

When Eben boarded the *Merrimack* later that day, he looked at once for Jamie but didn't see him. It was nearly a half hour before his classmate came over to him at his gun. When Jamie came, he was frowning—but not a frown of rage. It was worry.

Motioning Eben to follow him, the boy went to the farthest corner of the gun deck. Here he sat down and after a while said, "Eben, I haven't told anybody at all, but last night I woke up from sleeping when I heard a strange noise. It was kind of like somebody had dropped something on the deck. I didn't call out.

I stayed in the dark, and I'm sure glad I did." He took a deep breath. "I saw three men hunkered down by the lamp in front of the powder magazine. I couldn't tell who they were because their backs were to me. I heard them whispering, though. They drew lines with their fingers on the deck. Then the one in the middle said, 'Tomorrow night, for sure. We'll do it right here. That'll be the end of her.' After that, they left. They never knew I was there listening in."

Eben was silent, thinking.

Jamie spoke again. "I don't know what to do. I could have misunderstood what they said, but I don't think so. I've thought it over and over. I think me and you oughta stay in the powder magazine tonight and see what they're up to. I think maybe they're planning to blow up our ship, because they're coming down to the powder magazine. If we can't stop them from doing that, we can still get clear. All we got to do is follow them out as they go."

"Jamie, maybe we ought to tell Gunner Kendrick or Mr. Brooke or Lieutenant Jones," said Eben. "But wait a minute. That might not be such a dandy idea, though. You're new here, and I'm only a powder-monkey, even if I've been aboard longer. We could be laughed at—or ordered off the gun deck—for this if we're wrong. We don't have proof." After a moment, Eben added, "All right, I'm gonna ask Zekiel Preston—you know him, the powderboy of the other six-incher—to row over and tell Ma that I'm staying on board tonight. You and I'll keep watch together down in the magazine. Ma won't like it, but I'll just have to try and talk her out of her being mad later on. She's been mad a lot lately. I guess it's because she misses Pa so much. I'm going to stay with you."

Four bells in the mid-watch meant 10 P.M. to Eben. He whispered the landlubber's time to Jamie as they huddled in the cramped, uncomfortable powder magazine. They had sneaked down there unseen after they'd been dismissed from their gun crews that afternoon.

Neither of them dared to fall asleep. They had to stay awake! The hours passed. Eight bells—midnight—sounded. The *Merrimack* was silent. The last roving guard had made his final rounds, and the whale-oil lights burned low and smelled badly.

Two bells—one o'clock in the morning. The boys' eyes had become very heavy, yet still there was no motion and no sound. The flannel-covered powder bags had been soft beneath them to start with, but now they felt as if they were full of rocks. However, they dared not move for fear of making a noise. At five bells, two-thirty in the morning, there came a sound. At last!

Eben and Jamie sat breathlessly watching as three men came walking, crouched over. They were shrouded with long dark coats and they carried lighted candles with them as they moved slowly in the bottom of the silent ship.

As the boys looked on, one of the men reached into the powder locker and withdrew three powder bags. His hand missed Eben's foot by only a few inches, and if he hadn't been partially blinded by the candle flame, he would have seen the boy. Walking back, he placed the three bags next to the hull planking of the ship and then tied them together with a double knot. Tugging the fuse to make sure the knot had jammed tight and could not be pulled loose, he wedged the charge tightly into the corner where the ship's rib touched the planking. Once more he pulled the fuse. The charge only jammed tighter. Satisfied, he ran the fuse to a point in the middle of the ship and lit it from the candle.

A voice that Eben recognized with a thrill of horror spoke firmly. "We'll blow her sky-high, lads. A hole in her side and a fire started by the gunpowder will mean her end. The *Merrimack* will never go out to fight. It'll take only a few minutes after the explosion before the powder magazine goes up. Fewer lives will be lost and *our* ship will be invincible."

His voice had betrayed him. This was Jack Rawlins! Furious at the extent of the man's treachery, Eben wanted to shout out his name, accusing him, but immediately thought better of it. He and Jamie were only boys, no match for the three men, and there was nobody near enough to hear their cries this far belowdecks.

Silently, biting his lip and holding his temper to save his life, Eben gripped Jamie's sweaty hand to keep him silent, too. They waited.

Rawlins's work was swiftly done. The men waited to see that the fuse burned properly and then left as silently as they had come.

The minute they had disappeared into the blackness of the lower deck, Jamie wanted to run over and put out the fuse. Counting off seconds in his head, Eben held him back with his hand. They *had* to wait! They had to make sure Rawlins and his friends did not decide to return and check their handiwork. Eben knew they would still have time to abandon ship if they couldn't defuse the charge.

Three minutes went by, every second seemingly endless while the boys watched the sputter of the fuse as it carried fire slowly to the charge. At times, nothing was visible of it, then a spurt of flame would come up as the pitch-coated linen cover burned through. Looking carefully, Eben calculated it was burning about a foot a minute as it traveled toward the charge that would destroy his ship.

At the start of the fourth minute, the boys broke from their cover and raced to the sputtering cord. It would be easy to cut it with a knife, but neither had one because of safety rules. Anything that could possibly spark was kept well clear of the powder magazine. Eben dived to the corner and touched the charge. It was stuck tight; he couldn't get his fingers behind it to pull it out. He grabbed the fuse and pulled with all his might. It would not come loose, either. In fact, he could feel that the charge had jammed even tighter.

"I'll try to untie it, Jamie," he whispered loudly, and then dropped to his knees. He groped in the darkness for the knot. Soon he had it, and a feeling of relief came over him—all he had to do was to untie it. Just as quickly, however, there came an icy chill as he realized the knot was rock-hard. For a second, Eben sat back on his knees. Now he was frightened and bewildered, and his sideward glance showed him that the burning fuse was very close. He knew there was not enough time to escape. It was do or die!

He looked in desperation to Jamie and saw him on his knees, too. He had the fuse in his mouth and was furiously chewing on it. Eben realized that this was their only hope. Just maybe they could cut the fuse with their teeth or wet the black powder inside the fuse with saliva to stop the burning. Quickly, he joined Jamie, chewing the fuse close to the charge. He looked up as he heard a gasp of pain. Jamie's face had been burned and he had dropped the fuse. In just seconds, it burned past the spot where Jamie had been chewing it and raced on toward Eben.

Now it was up to Eben. If there was pain, he would have to withstand it. Jamie had been taken by surprise; he couldn't let this happen to him. Every bit of saliva Eben had in his fear-dried mouth was chewed into the tough covering of the fuse. He had to wet that powder and stop the flame or just maybe weaken the fuse so it could be pulled apart.

A spurt of fire singed his face. Reacting to the sharp pain of the burn, he clenched his teeth and jerked his head back. Nothing happened. Now he felt the fire at his lips—how it hurt! He kept chewing, the fire was touching his teeth and would soon be inside his mouth. The pain was too much; he lunged backward with all his strength, only to fall over and spit out the torn end of the fuse. His chewing had weakened the fuse and it had come apart. The fire was out.

"Eben, Eben, are you all right?" It was Jamie by his side, his smoke-scarred face next to Eben's. "I'm sorry, Eben. I couldn't hold the fuse; the fire surprised me more than it hurt. Are you all right?"

"Yes, I guess I am, Jamie," Eben said as he ran his tongue over his seared lips. "If I hadn't seen you, I wouldn't have known what to expect. I just hung on and chewed." Then he added, "It was you who did the right thing. You were quick and you knew we couldn't stomp that fuse out. We're real shipmates, all right."

Sitting back, the boys slowly realized what they'd just accomplished.

Eben told his friend, "I hope we can still spit straight after this. I bet those stinking Yankees are off somewhere watching to see our ship blow up."

Jamie was able to laugh through his burned lips. "They got a long time to wait then, Eben." He punched Eben in the side. "Together we could rassle a bear."

Eben laughed at this, then said, "Let's go up on deck and stay awake the rest of the night. We won't tell the guards. They wouldn't believe you and me. Tomorrow we'll tell Gunner Kendrick and the officer of the day what we saw. If old Rawlins tries to come back down here to the powder magazine, we'll yell for the guards. Let him sit where he is and wait and wait and wonder what went wrong. He won't like that one bit." Eben sighed. "I sort of liked him once. He was nice to me."

"He was nice to me, too, Eben. He talked to me today."

"I hate him now!" vowed Eben. "I really do. For what he tried to do to our ship."

The boys sat together on the top deck of the *Merrimack* until they saw the officer of the watch on the dock. Then they ran to meet him and make their report. Five minutes later, the man was down in the powder magazine with them, listening and examining the spot where the explosive charge had been set. A quick inspection proved their story. There were burned spots on the deck where the fuse had spurted fire.

While they talked with the officer of the watch, Gunner Kendrick came down the companionway.

He listened as the officer asked Eben, "Were the men who tried to set the charges engineers or were they from the gun deck?"

"The gun deck, Sir," said Eben.

"Were they?" exploded Kendrick. "Who were they?"

"Jack Rawlins and some men from the other guns," growled Eben in fury.

"Rawlins?" exclaimed Kendrick in amazement. "Are you sure?"

"We sure are. Jamie knows him, too. He's a dirty Yankee traitor."

Eben and Jamie told their story once again and showed Kendrick their burned mouths. When they were through, the gunner went with them and saw the same burn scars on the deck they had shown before. After examining the marks, the gun captain went over to the charge and looked at it. "Setting this," he said, "was the work of an experienced gunner, and Rawlins is that!"

While the officer of the watch went to inspect the engines, gear boxes, and boilers for damage and the coal bunkers for more explosives, Kendrick told the boys, "We have to report this to Mr. Brooke right now. You lads did mighty well. We're going to hold a muster of the gun crews, and I'll count noses. I just bet that there'll be three cannoneers missing and that Rawlins will be one of them."

Mr. Brooke was on the gun deck. After he heard out the boys' and Kendrick's short explanation, he nodded as Kendrick called out, "Gun crews, fall in back of your cannon. Gun captains, count your men and report to me."

The report was swiftly made. Three men were missing: Rawlins, Henry Bell, and Isaac Allen. Now Brooke called the ship's disciplinary officer and asked him to send out teams of guards to find the missing men, although he realized the chances of catching them were slim. If they had fast horses ready or a boat stowed along the shore waiting for them, they would be safe with other Union men by now. They had had some hours to get away once they had seen their plot had failed.

Brooke told Eben and Jamie, "You're good lads. I'm proud of you for what you did to save the ship for the South. See the doctor and get some salve for your lips."

He next turned to the gun captain and asked, "Mr. Kendrick, what do you know about Rawlins? I recall that you picked him out, and it seemed to me that you knew him well. Didn't the two of you serve together somewhere on some other vessel?"

"Aye, Sir, that we did." The master gunner spoke

slowly. "We were shipmates on the old *Savannah.* Twenty-four guns she carried. It was back in 1859. That was off Tripoli in Mediterranean waters. Rawlins was always a good hand then, able and willing; but, you know, I never did quite figure him out. He didn't talk much, and even when he did, he didn't ever say anything to really get hold of. It was kind of like he was keeping a secret from everybody."

"How was that?"

"First of all, it was how he came aboard the *Savannah.* He didn't ship out of Boston like the rest of the crew. He was rowed out to her from Tripoli and he was wearing handcuffs. He was taken to the captain's cabin but was back out on deck fast as he went in, with the captain yelling after him." Kendrick shook his head. "We learned later on that he spat at the captain. Anyhow, he was in irons for quite a time after that and was flogged. Later on, he became part of my gun crew. He told me once he was a Marylander from Baltimore. Maybe that was true, maybe not. He didn't ever talk like a Yankee. He worked hard and with a will, but I never did find out what had happened to him in Tripoli. He never complained, not him . . . and he never talked about his life or his troubles. As I said, he didn't ever say much, but he sure listened a lot. Sometimes I thought he felt he was better than the rest of us and was laughing at us, but he did his seaman's duty fair weather or foul, Sir."

It was Brooke's turn to be silent. A half minute went by as he looked scowling at the scrubbed gun deck, then he said, "I doubt that what seemed to you to happen in Tripoli was the truth. From what you say, Gunner, my opinion is that this Rawlins was never a prisoner. I believe he was a Union Navy officer put aboard the *Savannah* in foreign waters to find out about Southern affairs from her crew. All this took place about a year and a half before we Confederates fired on Fort Sumter in South Carolina. The North knew war was brewing then, and assuredly would have sent out spies to gather information." Brooke sighed. "Well, now that Rawlins and the other two have gotten away, and I'm positive they have, we can be sure the Yankees will know everything about the *Merrimack* very soon—if Rawlins hasn't told them everything before this time. If it's true that the Yankees are building their own ironclad ship, this news will spur them on. That means we've got to work around the clock to get ready to attack the blockaders before we lose the advantage we may still have."

"Cuss all Yankees to damnation!" Eben muttered between his teeth.

With the knowledge that they could have lost the secret of their ship, the crew now labored furiously to get her ready. In three days' time, the water doors to the dry dock were opened. Eben and Jamie watched from the dockside as the water inched its way up the *Merrimack*'s keel and then finally hid the keel as it went up past the bilges and along the sides. In just two hours, enough water had entered so that the gun deck was close to the water. But would a ship with so much iron float? Eben asked himself the question anxiously.

The water continued creeping up the sides of the ship until there was less than a foot of the hull remaining dry. Oh, Lord, thought Eben, she's going to sink right here at the dock. At the very moment he despaired of ever seeing the *Merrimack* float, however, a gentle movement of her hull showed that her keel had lifted from its blocks. In another minute, the wooden blocks floated to the surface alongside her hull.

A loud cheer of joy rose from the men lining the sides of the dry-dock rampart as they saw their ship floating. Like the two powderboys, they looked on in rapt silence as the cheering died away. Turning to Jamie, Eben stuck out his hand. Clasping hands in a firm handshake, the two Virginia boys stood together admiring their ship.

Eben Tyne, who had hung about his ship for weeks waiting and continuing to work at the navy yard, officially reported for duty on the seventh of March—some days after the *Merrimack*'s silver-haired captain,

Franklin Buchanan, took over the command. Jamie was waiting for him at the bottom of the rampart steps where he moored the skiff. Jamie shouted excitedly, "The crew's all aboard, Eben! Engine fires are starting up tonight and tomorrow we're gonna go out on the river for a trial run. We're to stand to our guns like it's a real battle!"

"Out on the river?" Eben whistled. Now they would finally learn how the *Merrimack* would handle herself. She was mighty big and heavy—the heaviest thing that had ever floated on any sea in the history of the world.

Eben's heart swelled with pride! He would go out with his ship. How he wished Pa and Jason and his pa could see her leave for the bay!

That evening after supper, Eben sat with his mother at the kitchen table, enjoying the welcome warmth of the stove after a cold March day at the navy yard. Proudly, Eben told her, "Ma, the *Merrimack*'s going out on the river tomorrow. It'll be her first run."

"Is she now, Eben?" Mrs. Tyne's gaze was level. She didn't smile.

He went on excitedly, "We want to see how her engines work. They're kinda old."

"Are they?"

"Yeah, we had to fix them up plenty, they were in such bad shape."

Mrs. Tyne was embroidering a sampler. She moved

closer to the coal-oil lamp on the table to see better and said, "Son, I don't want you to go out on that ship tomorrow."

"Not go?" Eben blurted out in a wail of amazement.

"You heard what I said. You went out on the *Lucy* with your father, and I sat here waiting, praying all night long. You've practiced being a powderboy on the *Merrimack* long enough. You could have been killed when those Northern spies tried to blow her up. You think I didn't hear about that? People in Norfolk talk, you know. They congratulated me on what a fine, brave lad you are! Your father's gone, and there's been no word from him, or from Jason's father, either. You know the South does not take the only son of a family for a soldier or a sailor. I don't want you going over to the *Merrimack* again. After all, you didn't take any oath to join the Confederate Navy the way adult seamen do, did you?"

Eben cried out angrily, "But this isn't a fair thing for you to do! They need me."

Calmly, Mrs. Tyne pulled red thread through the cloth with a ripping sound. "I need you, too, Eben. Have you ever given a thought to anyone or anything lately but that ship? All there is to you is that ironclad. Oh, yes, you do your chores each day and you help Mrs. Owens, but your mind's only on that ship."

"Ma, she's going to bust the blockade!"

"Then she can do that without you. You did enough

aboard the *Lucy*. Some other boy can do your work. I've already given up my husband. I won't give up my son!"

"Ma, there's just one powdermonkey to each cannon. They need me!"

"I don't care about that, Eben. Anyone can carry a bag of powder, can't he? I am for the South as much as you are, but think what this war is like for the women. Men die in battle, and we are left behind to be widows and to care for orphans. We get no glory. We get to take care of wounded husbands, sons, and brothers, and to bury them if the bodies are ever sent home to us. We wait and suffer in silence. Your father may never come home to me. Sea voyages are dangerous at any time—in wartime doubly so. Yankee privateer ships roam the Atlantic. I will not risk losing you, too.

"I have a bad feeling about this trial run of yours. I don't like it at all. I will be heard in this matter. I'll send a message to your gun crew chief, that Kendrick you talk about so much, and let him know I need you here at home more than he does. I think I should be considered, too! You did your duty by the South on the *Lucy*. I won't hear any argument from you! Get up to bed at once, Eben Tyne."

Eben knew that his mother meant every word she had said. She had had her speech ready and waiting for a long time. When Amanda Tyne gave an order, she expected it to be obeyed. She was like his pa that way, but Pa would understand. How Eben wished he were here now!

Realizing that he could not reason with his mother—only obey her—Eben slowly and furiously stomped up the stairs to his room and went inside. He could hear his mother's footsteps a moment later as she came up behind him with the lamp. Instead of passing by his room, he heard her stop. Then he heard the clink of a key turn in the lock of his door. *She had locked him in.*

Blast it! She meant to keep him locked in all day long tomorrow and send her message. Gunner Kendrick would certainly be disgusted with him and her. Not just *anybody* could carry a bag of gunpowder and know what he was doing.

Eben fumed. He flung himself onto his bed, thinking of her words. Well, there was some justice in them, but she just didn't understand. Now that he looked back, he recalled how frightened she had often looked when he had told her some of what went on aboard the ironclad. She had only been biding her time. What would his gun crew do without him? His cannon would be useless, that fine gun he had rifled himself.

No, it wouldn't. Be damned if it would!

Eben got up, his face working angrily. Noiselessly, he opened his window and quietly crawled through it out onto the roof. He scrambled across it on his belly, turned to grab the overhang, and dropped to the ground. He made a thud, but not so loud that it would attract his mother's attention.

It was cold outside. His jacket was in the kitchen on its hook, but he knew that door was locked. Well, he would warm up by running hard, and he would row hard, too, to the yard. He could sleep again with Jamie in the powder magazine and share his blankets.

He wasn't going to miss his ship's first venture out into the river. He just had to go! It was what Captain Sam Tyne would want. Why else would he have taken Eben to the navy yard? His pa wanted him to do this!

CHAPTER NINE

BATTLE STATIONS

Passing the *Merrimack*'s guards, Eben went down to the powder magazine. Settling in, he awakened Jamie, who asked sleepily, "What're you doing here, Eben?"

"Go back to sleep. I came over early. I couldn't sleep at home, so I decided to row over here." No, he wouldn't tell Jamie what his ma had done to him. There was no telling what Jamie would say—he might feel sorry for him or he might tease him. He wanted neither reaction.

The eighth of March dawned brightly. The last test of the ship's engines had been made and her steering checked over. Today the *Merrimack* would go out on the Elizabeth River, steam around, and come back to the dock for final adjustments. Maybe tomorrow she'll go out and fight in earnest was the ship rumor!

Excitedly, Eben went to his gun station to hear the long-awaited command passed along to the gun crew: "Cast off, fore and aft." When it came, Eben's heart beat faster. He felt the gentle vibrations of the deck as the moving propeller bit into the water. They were finally going out! Grinning, he stood ready behind his gun, even though he knew this was just another trial.

As the warship moved down the mouth of the river where it opened into the bay, the *Merrimack*'s captain, Franklin Buchanan, surveyed the scene around him. Straight ahead of his ship were five big Federal vessels swinging at anchor. The *Cumberland* and the *Congress* were closest to the *Merrimack*. Farther off were two sister ships to the *Merrimack* when she had been part of the Federal Navy—the *Minnesota* and the *Roanoke*. A little farther along the line, sitting peacefully on the smooth, misty waters, was the *St. Lawrence*. All together, these ships carried more than two hundred guns, and that didn't count the shore batteries that could be brought to bear on the lone Confederate ship. Cannonwise, the odds against the *Merrimack* were nearly twenty-five to one.

Her battle-wise commander took all of this in at a glance. His glance also showed him that today was laundry day in the Yankee fleet. Sailors' clothing and blankets had been strung in the ships' rigging to dry. Just possibly, many crew members might be on shore where the Yankees held territory.

He reached a crucial decision. "Helmsman, turn to port and lay near to Craney Island," he ordered. "Mr. Jones, have the workmen aboard this ship assembled. We're going to put them ashore. Then we'll get down to business."

Through his open gunport, Eben saw the workmen leave as the *Merrimack* slowed down to two knots. A lifeboat was slung over the side and the men piled into it to row ashore. Why do this, he wondered?

Once they were away, the captain gave another order. "Helmsman, hard a starboard. Your course is to that enemy sloop of war across the bay, the *Cumberland!*"

Now the *Merrimack* made her final test turn, pointing her iron beak at the enemy frigate. Coal was shoveled into her fireboxes, and with a heavy black cloud of smoke coming from her funnel, she raised a wave at her bow as she charged at her full six-knot speed— the speed a man could trot—into Norfolk Bay on her way to battle.

"Mr. Jones, clear the ship for action! Run up the colors!" Immediately, the captain's orders sounded through the ship as they were relayed from gun captain to gun captain and to the engine room. Eben stood gasping. "Clear the ship for action!" "Run up the colors" on a *trial* run?

Now he heard cheering at a distance. From his gunport, he saw that the riverbanks were lined with men in gray, Confederate artillery and infantry. They had come to see the ironclad's trial run, but as soon as they saw her colors run up and flying proudly, they knew this wasn't to be a trial run. They knew the reason for her surging speed. They tossed their caps into the air and cheered again and again. Their strong, hard voices carried the strains of "Dixie" to the ship as she steamed past.

Just as the soldiers watched his ship, Eben Tyne watched them. His heart beating rapidly, he waved back, returning the greeting, though he doubted they could see his arm coming out of the gunport.

It was several minutes before the crew fully understood what was really happening aboard the *Merrimack* and what Captain Buchanan meant to do. First they wondered whether the drill with colors was just a ruse to try them out as well as test their skill and courage. Then, with the constant flapping of their battle flag overhead, they realized an actual fight was about to take place!

This was real! Victory or defeat would come from what they did today.

As if on order, a single lusty cheer went up from the *Merrimack* crew. Then it was check and recheck each item aboard to make sure it was ready for action. Shot was placed in the racks and the shot cage was filled. Eben, Jamie, and the other powdermonkeys, passing one another, made their trips to the powder magazine and filled their powder lockers with eight charges each.

As the decks were cleared for action and the powder brought up to serve the guns, the captain of the *Merrimack* signaled to the two small gunboats at his side to accompany his ship. Cheers came from the crews of the *Raleigh* and the *Beaufort* as they took up their positions. If there was going to be a fight, they would be in it, too.

With the gunports still open and the guns "served," Eben watched the small ships move alongside his ship. He felt an uncontrollable, trembling excitement. It was the *Lucy* once again! His body felt alive as it had felt only once before, for that short time aboard the little paddle-wheeler. He tingled all over.

Feeling like a skittish horse, he looked down the rows of cannon on his gun deck and saw Jamie doing a small dance of nervousness. Then Eben noticed that the gun crews were also somehow different. Tom Kendrick, the veteran gunner, seemed to move more quickly and with more authority than ever before, going from man to man among his crews, speaking to and touching each one on the shoulder. Eben felt a mixture of excitement and righteous wrath against the enemy, of extreme danger, and yet he felt confidence in himself. There was no word for this sensation. It was not to be named. This was not like being aboard the *Lucy.*

"Close gunports!" came the passed-along command aboard the *Merrimack,* and Tom Kendrick ordered Eben's viewing place closed. From now on, the gun crews would work in the dim light from the overhead grating.

Suddenly, Eben heard and felt something hit the ironclad side of the *Merrimack*—one great thudding bang after another. Cannon fire. They were being fired on!

The shots bounced off the slanted sides of the *Merrimack* like raindrops on a windowpane, their clangs as they hit the armor deafening the gun crews. The scream of the shells as they ricocheted and ran off into space made Eben's hair rise up when he heard them for the first time. No, this was not one bit like being fired on aboard the *Lucy.* It was a thousand times worse. Eben's bow gun was on the side being pounded by the Federal gunship, the *Zouave.* Each impact sent shock waves that hit him like punches to the body. His one thought was, Would the gunports hold? He prayed that they would.

After firing six rounds, the *Zouave* stopped. Why fire only to have cannonballs bounce off the target?

There was action aboard the *Merrimack* now.

Quickly, her officers made an inspection of the ship and found that no real damage had been done. Knowing the strength of his ship, Captain Buchanan sent signals to the *Raleigh* and *Beaufort* to return to port. They were no match for the Union guns, and he didn't want them lost and their crews killed. With a salute of their whistles, the little ships veered off to return to Norfolk.

The attack of the *Zouave* and the slow speed of *Merrimack* gave the Yankee blockaders plenty of time to pull in their laundry from their rigging and to prepare for battle. Cleared for action, their cannon loaded and primed, the ships aligned themselves to greet the oncoming Confederate ironclad. As soon as she came into range, the fifty-gun *Congress* fired a twenty-five-gun broadside at her simultaneously.

Eben Tyne found the din almost unbearable. The *Merrimack* rocked from the impact of nearly a ton and a half of metal hitting her all at the same time. He was knocked to his knees. Those on the other side where the broadside hit were already bleeding from their noses as the heavy concussion burst the tiny veins in their noses. They shook their heads as they came to their feet. A sailor lay quiet mid-deck as if dead. He was a cannoneer who had placed his shoulder at the side of the casement and had been thrown halfway across the ship by the impact of the cannonball that had hit the armor just on the other side from him. No one ran to pick him up—gun crews were to stand by their guns.

Not having fired one cannon yet, the *Merrimack* continued on her course toward the *Cumberland,* only to receive another full broadside from the *Congress* at much closer range. Eben and the others of her crew were ready for this one, but it was even worse than the first. The shells struck with greater force. This time, Union field artillery from the shore batteries joined in firing at the *Merrimack.*

Eben, his voice breaking shrilly with tension and repressed impatience, cried to Kendrick, "When will we shoot? Isn't it time for *us* to shoot?"

"Easy!" shouted Kendrick in turn. "We're getting into position. It'll be soon." The gunner could scarcely be heard above the awful clamor.

Though the waiting was only minutes, to Eben it felt forever. This anvil-like crashing of cannonballs striking his ship was unnerving. He began to anticipate the next shot. Moving to straighten a powder charge that had fallen over, he neared the ship's hull. As he knelt, a solid shot hit her iron casement just over his head. Quickly, he picked himself up from the deck where he had been thrown by the concussion. His head was ringing and he had a nosebleed. He remembered to keep his mouth open and to breathe through it to equalize the pressure on his eardrums. If he hadn't done instinctively what his gun captain had told his crew over and over to do, both of Eben's eardrums would have been ruptured.

At last came the shouted command "Starboard battery, gunports up! Guns run out!" Up went the gunport shields, out pushed the black muzzles of the big six-inch guns.

Through his open gunport, Eben saw the black-painted hull of a ship only yards away.

"Fire!" came the command. Flame and smoke belched from the *Merrimack*'s cannon as they hurled their shots into the side of the *Congress*. A roar of relief came up from the crews frustrated by waiting. Eben's own high yell was lost in all the shouting. Now the Yankees knew the *Merrimack* had a bite.

Next came the command "In haul! Gunports down!" In came the guns and down went the iron shutters. Spongemen leaped to swab out the bores of their cannons. Then, like machinery that worked in unison, the crews reloaded their pieces.

Now the *Merrimack*'s cannon fell silent as the rain of Union shells became heavier. The clamor of their exploding was deafening. Eben saw that, just as he had been told to expect, the visibility on his gun deck was getting poorer and poorer. Soon the gunners would have to work by feel. This was why everything had to be in its *exact* place constantly. Some of the gun crews in an area that couldn't be ventilated by fresh sea air were already vomiting from the sulfur smoke of burned gunpowder. The overhead grating did little good because the heavy smoke held low to the gun deck.

"Port side, gunports up! Guns run out!" came the command from the opposite side of the ship. The *Merrimack* had changed her course to bring these guns to bear now, and the Yankees were going to get her shots from the left side. A blast of fire answered the command. A heavy cloud of smoke rose up, and this time the rending, grinding sound of splintered wood was clearly heard as the *Cumberland* was pierced by the *Merrimack*'s broadside.

Hit low in the water, the *Cumberland* was going to sink, but she was not going to surrender. Another broadside was fired into her, and then the Confederate ironclad slammed into the sinking ship, burying her beak just under the *Cumberland*'s foremast, punching a huge hole through it.

Though sweating, Eben felt a chill run up his spine when he heard the screech from the broken wood as his ship's ram pushed right through the *Cumberland*'s hull. Anything that was loose on his gun deck was thrown toward the bow of the ship. Gun crews held on to their hot cannon for support and grabbed for their swab buckets to catch hold of them as they slid along the deck.

Suddenly, Eben realized with horror that not only was the *Cumberland* sinking but that the *Merrimack* was, too! She didn't have the steam power to pull her ram free from the stricken enemy. So while the *Cumberland* took on tons of water and began tilting to her watery grave, his ship was forced deeper and deeper into the bay at the same time.

Then a sound like yet another cannon shot was heard. But it wasn't! It was the *Merrimack*'s cast-iron beak breaking off at the bow to stay rammed deep in the side of the Yankee ship. With a gentle bob of her massive bow, the Confederate ship floated free.

Called on to surrender, the captain of the *Cumberland* refused. Although mortally wounded, his ship fought back, firing on the *Merrimack* as long as her guns stayed above water.

As the firing slackened off from the *Cumberland,* the gun crews of the *Merrimack* were able to risk looking out of their gunports. They watched the *Cumberland* go down, her colors still flying, fighting to the very last.

A cheer went up from the *Merrimack*'s gun deck to honor their victory, but it ceased as suddenly as it had started, except for Eben's own "hurrah." Men turned to stare at him until he stopped, too. He realized why they were so somber. Brave men had died there over the water. All at once, Eben knew that you do not cheer in war. Its sheer brutality is too overwhelming. One minute, the *Cumberland* had been a splendid ship, the next a sinking, shell-riddled hulk carrying her dead to their silent graves.

Pulling away from her, Captain Buchanan ordered a new course. This time, it was toward the nearby frigate, the *Congress,* nearest in line to the sunken *Cumberland.*

Knowing what was coming, the young captain of the U.S.S. *Congress* had slipped his ship's anchor chain and made sail to get away before the enemy ironclad turned from the doomed *Cumberland.* As he tried to maneuver his ship, she ran aground in the shallow waters of the bay. With no option but to fight, the *Congress* unloaded broadside after broadside on the *Merrimack.*

A cannon duel began anew—this time even fiercer than before. The *Congress* carried heavier guns than her sister ship, and she could bring them to bear on the *Merrimack.* The din of shot striking on the iron plates of the Confederate ship was so loud that gunners' orders could not be heard. Firing was done not in any coordinated sense but at the will of the individual gun captains—and not by words but by gestures. Nearly everyone serving the guns had nosebleeds. Many bled at the ears, too, and were shaking their heads to try to clear the confusion in their brains, only to be sickened again by the concussion of the next shot.

Mechanically, the crews served their guns. The drilling of Tom Kendrick and the other gun captains was paying off. Without the steel they had placed in their men, the gun crews of the *Merrimack* would be falling from exhaustion. They worked on without a letup. Eben, Jamie, and the other powderboys walked with smoke-filled eyes and searing lungs to make trip after trip down to the powder magazine. In the fury of the fight, they lost count of the times they had gone up and down the steps to fetch powder and water. Coughing in the smoke, they carried buckets of water to their guns, where the cannoneers drank it, then sloshed themselves to be able to go on fighting.

Everyone's face was soot-covered by the foul-smelling gunpowder smoke. Men had white lines carved through the layer of soot where their eyes kept shedding tears to clear themselves from the irritation. More than anything in the world right now, Eben Tyne, like his shipmates, wanted a lungful of fresh sea air.

In this new battle, the thick smoke began filtering down the companionways to the lower decks, sucked there by the engines' need for air. Constantly fed by the firing above, the smoke got thicker and thicker. Eben saw the hooded lamps at the entrance of the powder magazine as just glimmers in the darkness. Everything men did was now done by touch only. Breathing became a painful rasping as lungs labored to get the oxygen they must have. Slipping, sometimes bumping into each other, the powdermonkeys carried on.

The *Merrimack* steamed to nearly two hundred

yards from the stranded *Congress*. To go any closer could mean grounding the ironclad, too. From that point, her cannons pounded the enemy. Flame and smoke shrouded the combatants as broadside after broadside was exchanged. This time, it was the *Merrimack* that suffered. The crews of the numbers 2 and 3 Dahlgrens on the port side were hit while their gunports were open to fire. Blood flowed over the deck as the wounded men lay where the shells' impact had thrown them.

Eben's heart almost stopped as the news was passed down to his gun. Jamie served the number 3 gun! Was he all right? If only he could leave his own gun to see, but Eben dared not!

When the *Merrimack*'s gun crews had all but believed the fighting could not be worse, a new surge of activity took place. Sweating bodies swabbed, loaded, and fired their cannon as if the very devil was after them. For a short period, the deck was frantic with movement. It was as though the very last ounce of the men's energy was being used in a final spurt for victory. The *Merrimack* shot one broadside after another into the Yankee frigate until the *Congress*, now a wreck, lowered her colors and ran up the flag of surrender.

As soon as he saw that flag, Captain Buchanan ordered, "Cease firing." His gun crews readied their cannons, set their equipment back in the exact places, and then, at last, slumped exhaustedly to the decks, lying where they fell.

Eben didn't stay at his gun now. He scuttled, rather than walked, to the number 3 gun to find Jamie. Thank the Lord, his friend was all right. Jamie lay on his back, unwounded on the bloody deck. He gasped as he took Eben's hand, but he grinned, his teeth white in his soot-blackened face. "I be fine," he croaked.

Gunner Kendrick didn't let his men rest long. Soon he sang out, "All right, on your feet! Keep moving. Take it easy, but move! We ain't out of this fight yet. If I need you, I don't want you stove-up."

The men got back to their feet.

The *Merrimack* surged against the tide to come to a full stop, standing by to take prisoners off the *Congress.* Some of her crew were ordered out onto the top deck to receive these defeated Yankees. Suddenly, the commander of the Yankee field artillery on shore ordered his guns to open fire on the unsuspecting *Merrimack.* The *Congress* may have surrendered, but he had not!

From where he stood, Eben heard the whistling of incoming rounds of artillery fire. The men on his ship's upper deck dived for protection, but two of the *Merrimack's* lieutenants were killed outright. Captain Buchanan was wounded.

Thinking that the *Congress,* not the shore artillery, had fired treacherously on his ship after running up the white flag, the captain ordered red-hot cannon-balls to be loaded into the barrels. The reddish-white projectiles were fired at the crippled *Congress*. They started fires wherever they touched wood, and the ship was soon ablaze.

With the *Cumberland* sunk and the *Congress* afire, the other three Union ships joined the fight. As the *Merrimack* moved to meet them, the news about the *Congress* was passed to her gun crews belowdecks.

"Men, she's finished," reported Gunner Kendrick. "The *Congress* is done for and afire from stem to stern."

There was no cheering this time, either. The sounds below were of coughing and panting—that was all.

On order of Lieutenant Jones, who had taken over the command from the wounded Captain Buchanan, the *Merrimack* pulled away from the flaming frigate and pointed herself at the next ship of the line. The lieutenant knew now that his ship could withstand the cannon fire of any anchored vessel in the Union Navy, but if one of them rammed the Confederate ship, she would roll over and sink like a rock, straight down to Davy Jones's locker.

As the lieutenant sought to maneuver the *Merrimack* into position for the upcoming battle, a stroke of luck came to favor the Confederate ship. Hugging the north bank of the bay to stay out of range of the Confederate field artillery directly to their south, first the *Roanoke,* then the *St. Lawrence,* and finally the *Minnesota* ran aground in the dangerous shoal waters. But if Lieutenant Jones wasn't careful, the *Merrimack* would join them. The tide was racing out to sea, and the ironclad would soon be unable to move freely, or to come into close enough range to engage her grounded enemies.

The officer ordered, "Helm over," and steamed his ship back to her moorage at Gosport Navy Yard to unload the wounded and dead, repair her damage, and get ready to return to fight on the morning's full tide.

Eben sensed the ship's turning and wondered whether she was going to attack another Yankee vessel. When he learned that they were headed home for the day, he was too bone-weary to feel either disappointment or relief at their retreat. Suddenly worn-out completely, the boy slumped to the deck and lay there, and this time Gunner Kendrick let him be.

· CHAPTER TEN ·

THE YANKEE SURPRISE

The *Merrimack* was tied up alongside the navy yard quay, and Eben watched from his gunport as the twenty-one wounded and dead of his ship were carried off. He was saddened to see that the old captain was among the injured to leave the ship. As he stood looking on, a soot-streaked Jamie Sloat appeared at his elbow.

He yelled into Eben's ear, "They're brave 'uns, Eben! Our old captain was the best!"

"Aye, Jamie," Eben shouted back. "I'm glad you're all right."

"I was knocked out for a spell, but I'm fine now."

Gunner Kendrick now summoned the boys, and they returned to their duties. Tackle ropes had to be replaced with new ones, powder lockers filled, and shot racks refilled.

When they were finished, Eben and Jamie climbed out onto the upper deck. A surprise awaited them. Though the *Merrimack* had been fired on by more than one hundred cannon, her armor showed nothing more than dents where it had been struck.

As Eben followed Jamie around, he realized that they were yelling just as they had during the battle. Lowering his voice, Eben could hear well enough, even though his head still buzzed with the sounds of the explosions. Slowly, the boys' voice levels dropped as they looked about their ship.

The *Merrimack* appeared to have been cleaned by a giant broom. The railing, deck supports, and lifeboat stands had all been swept away by the gunfire. The great iron beak was broken off just at the bow, and one anchor had been shot away. The *Merrimack*'s funnel looked like Swiss cheese, and steam pipes were broken. Already workmen had boarded the ship to tighten the armor plates jolted loose from their bolts by cannon impact.

Their inspection finished, the two boys decided there was only one thing left to do now. Nodding to each other, they jumped over the side into the cold Elizabeth River, clothes and all. What they needed was a bath! One sailor after another joined them, until soon more than fifty men were splashing and playing in the water, happy simply to be alive. From the river, they could hear the church bells ringing in Norfolk to celebrate their victory.

The next day's dawn came, and once more the *Merrimack* sallied forth, repaired as best she could be in such a short period of time. She meant to destroy the Federal blockade today. Her crew, now veterans, was somberly ready, and all preparations for the fight were handled speedily. Then again it was "Stand to stations"—and wait!

Lieutenant Catesby ap Jones headed his ship directly for the frigate, *Minnesota*. But as the *Merrimack* closed on the stranded ship, a strange-looking little craft came out from behind the *Minnesota*'s hull. At first, she was thought to be a raft carrying one of the frigate's boilers to shore, but all at once she fired a shot! Eben, and everyone else on the *Merrimack,* thought an accidental explosion had taken place aboard it.

However, it was no explosion, no accident. Eben Tyne, peering through his open gunport, was looking at the U.S.S. *Monitor.* She had arrived during the night and had navigated herself to her present position by the flames of the *Congress,* which had burned like a torch in the darkness.

What an odd-looking little ship she was, thought Eben. She had no sails, but, like the *Merrimack*, was a steamer. Her deck was nearly at the sea line, and sitting on the middle of it was a round turret, looking like a big tin can. Compared to his ship, she looked like a toy boat, but she carried two great cannons, larger than the *Merrimack*'s. Aye, she was small but dangerous-looking, he decided. For sure, she was a Yankee ship. Could this be the rumored Federal ironclad?

Lieutenant Jones knew her for what she was and welcomed her into the bay with a broadside that screamed away from her turret as it ricocheted.

The day before, the superiority of iron over wood had been demonstrated. Today, it was to be iron against iron! The *Monitor* fired in return, and the first battle of ironclads began.

The two ships dueled on and on with cannon, each pounding the other with everything she could bring to bear.

Firing without letup, the Confederate ship gave the *Monitor* everything she had struck the wooden ships with earlier. Some gun captains put in extra powder charges to make their cannons harder-hitting, but these shots did no more damage to the Yankee ironclad than her long shots did to the *Merrimack*.

The sounds of the cannon firing and the concussions of impact as the *Monitor*'s 175-pound balls hit the *Merrimack*'s now-cracking iron armor plate made men who had stood the fight well enough the day before shudder and stagger. They bled freely from their noses and suffered broken eardrums. The gun deck became a sea of grayish-blue powder smoke. Even the strongest were gasping for breath and retching from inhaling the poisonous smoke. Here and there lay bodies, seamen who had done their best and had worked until they collapsed and slipped into unconsciousness. Breathing through his mouth, his chest aching, Eben mopped at his bleeding nose with his sleeves as he worked his way down to the powder magazine.

Two hours of steady firing emptied the *Monitor* of all her ammunition. She pulled back to the shallows to hoist more shot and powder to her gun deck. As she did so, the *Merrimack* moved nearer the stranded *Minnesota,* which sent a crashing broadside into her. To avenge that, Kendrick's crew put a shell into her from their rifle gun. Now the *Merrimack* turned to bring her broadside against the *Minnesota,* only to find that the *Monitor* had returned to the fray.

The two ironclads again hammered each other with all their might. Shots screamed in the air as they bounded off the ships' hulls and fell into the water thousands of yards away. Closer and closer, the warships fought, and, as they did, the *Monitor*'s cannonballs continued to crack the iron plating of the *Merrimack.*

Lieutenant Jones was desperate. He knew he would

have to try something else. He would attempt to ram and sink the *Monitor* with the remnants of his ship's beak. Just maybe that would do the job. Each time he tried to close with the smaller Yankee vessel, however, she sheared off. She was too fast for the slower-moving Confederate ship to catch.

Then throughout his ship, he gave the order "Cutlasses, pistols, and boarding pikes. Prepare to board the enemy!"

Now Eben and the other powderboys leaped to a different and thrilling tune. Down they sped to the lower deck, where the racks of arms were stored. Each boy pulled an armload of cutlasses from the racks and carried them to his gun crew. They made more trips for pistols and pikes, fine powder, and pistol balls.

While Eben rushed up and down, his heart thudding wildly with excitement, he wondered to himself whether the powderboys would fight, too. None of them was to get the chance, however. The *Merrimack* could not maneuver alongside the swifter, elusive *Monitor,* even though she was only yards away. Each time the Confederate ironclad tried to catch the *Monitor* with the broken ram, she missed.

For another two hours, the long fight went on. More and more cannoneers dropped at their roaring guns, only to get up again and fight doggedly once more. The *Monitor*'s cannons were having an effect as they continued to crack and break up the Confederate ship's armor plate, but blast away as they did, they couldn't penetrate her two-foot-thick oak sides and their pitch-pine backing.

The final attempt to board the Yankee vessel was made at midday. The *Merrimack* came close, but once again the little ship danced away in the nick of time. With the *Merrimack*'s funnel so riddled by shot that her engines could get little of the air they desperately needed to keep them going, the ship was forced to move very slowly.

As the tide of battle turned against the Southern ship, a shot by one of her cannons struck the pilothouse of the *Monitor,* wounding the Union captain in the face. The *Monitor* returned to the safety of the shallow waters to see what damage had been done, and the *Merrimack* steamed very slowly toward the deep water.

Before long, the tide changed and the Confederate ironclad was forced to retreat even farther toward the center of the bay. Catesby ap Jones ordered "Helm up," and the ship headed for Norfolk. She had to go back to port for repairs before her engines gave out. Ever so slowly, the *Merrimack* turned and moved at half-speed, then quarter-speed, to Gosport Navy Yard. The *Monitor* did not follow, but held her position in the middle of the bay, safe from the shore batteries of Confederate field artillery. Throughout that long day, she lay there, protecting the blockading fleet.

As for Eben, he sat breathing deeply beside his open

gunport. His aching head was between his knees, and his hands were over his still-ringing ears.

Through the smoke, he saw men weeping openly from disappointment. They were exhausted, but they hadn't wanted to withdraw. Nor did he, but, like them, he believed their ship would come back as soon as she could. The encouraging words *later on today* circulated hopefully from lip to lip. But Gunner Kendrick, who could hear the failing engines' laboring sounds, solemnly told his crew, "We won't go out again today."

After they had anchored in Norfolk Bay, the chief engineer was forced to make a report to his commander on the state of the engines. Looking grim, he said, "Sir, they're old and tired. What little power they had was taken out of them today. We're working on them now, but it'll take a week of work around the clock to fix them. I can't give you any guarantees then. Simply, Sir, our engines are almost gone. We must have new parts."

Lieutenant Jones ordered the necessary work to be kept up and asked the engineer for a list of repair parts needed. Supplies would have to be sent to the ship from Richmond, and that would take time.

So the waiting began.

The day after the engagement with the *Monitor,* Eben and Jamie sat on the upper deck eating their breakfast of corn bread with molasses topping. Tom Kendrick walked over to them and asked, "How are your ears now, lads?"

Eben pulled at the lobe of his left one and said, "This one hurts, and I don't hear so good out of either one of them."

Jamie answered now: "Both of mine hurt and my head aches. So does my chest—from the smoke."

"Well, those things will pass. You both did real fine yesterday. No boys could have done better. You're good gun-deck men."

"When'll our ship go out again? I hope it's real soon," said Eben, pleased at the praise.

"That's up to the master of the ship to decide, not me." Kendrick smiled. "Don't be such a fire-eater, Tyne. You grow hot under the collar too fast. The Bible says, 'Wrath shortens the life.' While there's a lull in the action, I think it'd be the right thing for the two of you to write your folks that you came through the battle all right. We may have to take our ship out at any time, so there's no shore leave. Since they live in Norfolk, it ain't as if they couldn't hear what was going on yesterday in the bay between our ship and the Yankee ironclad, so they must be worrying some."

Jamie told him proudly, "I bet you they heard us firing all the way to Washington."

"To Richmond maybe, but not so much farther,"

the gunner corrected him. "You know where to go to find paper and ink and envelopes?"

Jamie shook his head, then asked, "Are the other powderboys writing home, too?" Eben could see Jamie didn't want to.

"Aye, them that can write and got families. Those that can't write can get an officer to do it for them."

"How about you, Mr. Kendrick?" asked Eben.

The man laughed bitterly. "I haven't got any folks anymore. Cholera took them all when I was a boy."

"You've got us," said Jamie boldly.

The man nodded. "Aye, that's so, and my ship." He got up and left.

Jamie asked Eben, "Are you gonna write your ma?" Earlier that morning, Eben had told his friend how he had left her because she had locked him in.

Eben heaved a sigh. "I reckon so. She'll be fretting. I'll do it today. It'll be the first letter I ever wrote. How about you, Jamie?"

Finished with his corn bread, Jamie lay back on the grating enjoying the cool March sunshine. He thought for a while before replying, "I can write good as you, but my ma can't read, so why write?"

"Jamie, somebody'd read her what you wrote."

"If Ma ever took it to anybody to do that for her. Naw, I'm more like Gunner Kendrick than you, I guess."

Eben got up slowly. "I'll go get some paper and a

pen and write Ma now." He frowned. "While I'm at it, I think I'll write somebody else, too."

"Who'd that be?"

"Becky Owens."

"Jason's skinny, carrot-top sister?" Jamie made a sour face.

"Uh-huh, her. I'm gonna ask her to go tell your ma that you came through the fight just fine."

"Would she go? All right. Thank you, Eben."

Eben procured what he needed from an officer. Then, finding a place at the bow of the *Merrimack,* he proceeded to write a scrawling note to his mother. It came hard and slow, but he finally got down what he thought he wanted to say. His lips moving silently, he read it aloud:

Dear Ma,

I take pen in hand to say that maybe by now you heard about the big fight my ship had with that Yankee ironclad yesterday. Maybe you even heard it happening. I'm not one bit hurt. I'm fine as ever and I eat good here.

Our gunner says I did real good in that fight.

Please don't ask me to come home now. Nobody from our ship is getting any shore leave. I want to stay with my ship. Don't send anybody after me. If somebody comes and drags me back, I'll just run away again. I'm needed here. Becky can milk our cow good as I can.

Don't fret over me. I'm safer here on this iron ship than I'd be on any wooden one. I need to be here in case that Yankee ironclad comes steaming in to fight our ships at the docks. Nobody else can stand up to her excepting for this ship.

Pa would want me to do what I'm doing right now. You know I just turned fourteen, so I'm old enough. I hear tell drummer boys go to war younger than that, and I'm safer on my ironclad than they are on land.

You can write me here at the navy yard, but they won't let you come visit.

Hoping you are well and in good spirits.

Your loving son, Eben Tyne

He folded the letter into an envelope and sealed it.

The next letter went more rapidly.

Dear Becky,

I just now wrote my ma a letter. You know I ran away. I reckon you know the whole story from her. I reckon, too, you know why I had to go. I was needed bad here and had a special job to do to serve the South.

Please go visit Ma often and talk to her. Try to

get her to see my side of things. I reckon she needs some cheering up.

The scrap between our ship and the Yankee iron-clad wasn't fun for me. I don't look forward to going through that again, but if I got to, I will. It made me sick for a while—gave me headaches and hurt my ears, but I'm fine now. I'm doing what Pa and your pa and Jason would expect me to do. Maybe you do, too?

Would you go see Jamie Sloat's ma and tell her he's fine, too? We're friends now and I'd sure like it if you'd go.

I send fond greetings and wishes to your ma. I wish you could come visit me, but we got guards everywhere here now to keep folks out. Me and Jamie stay close to our ship all the time. Remember me kindly.

Respectfully yours,

Eben

He readied that letter, too, and took both to a ship's officer for mailing.

His duty done, a somber Eben stood atop the deck, looking out over the bay. He asked himself how long it would be before his ship steamed out after the rest of the Yankee blockaders and again matched her fire-power with the *Monitor*. This time, the *Merrimack* would carry cannonballs aplenty.

• • •

A week passed with the *Merrimack* at anchor waiting for repair parts. They were to come by railroad from Richmond, the capital of the Confederacy, seventy miles north of Norfolk on the James River. Some parts arrived. Others did not and were undoubtedly not available.

Two weeks later, the *Merrimack*'s engines were still not strong enough to take her into the eastern reaches of Norfolk Bay to fight. The blockade went on.

Every day was like the day before for Eben and Jamie and everyone else aboard the ironclad. They ate three times a day, ran through gun drills twice a day to keep in practice, and often walked about the navy yard.

One early April afternoon, when Eben and his friend returned from visiting shops and forges, Eben was hailed by Mr. Kendrick, who told him, "There's a sea chest come aboard for you, Tyne." He led the way to a green-painted chest set on the dock. It had the name E. TYNE painted on it in red.

Eben cried, "Hey, it's mine! Pa made it for me. Ma musta sent it!"

He knelt, lifted the lid, and looked inside. There he saw shirts and overalls, his good shoes, and his foul-weather gear. On top was a single sheet of paper. He opened it and read the words: "You need not be dirty, son. Come home. You'll be welcome. I love you."

Tears came to Eben's eyes as he closed the chest and put the note into his pocket.

He got up and heard Jamie say, "Well, you won't be so dirty-looking anymore, Eben."

Blinking away the tears, Eben told him, "I'll share with you what'll fit, Jamie, so you won't look so dirty anymore, either."

Kendrick laughed and pointed over the side of the ship. "There's water aplenty down there and soap for the asking and buckets if you want them. There's no cause to be dirty. The navy don't like dirt."

"Is that an order—to wash?" asked Jamie.

"You can both take it as one, lads. Wash yourselves while you're washing your shirts. Go out in the shallows and do it all standing up. That's the easy way."

Eben promised, "We'll do it today, Mr. Kendrick. Say, do you think we'll go out to fight again real soon?"

"I don't know, Tyne. It's up to our new captain."

Eben nodded. Captain Buchanan had left the *Merrimack* because of his wound and had been replaced by tall, long-armed gray-bearded Josiah Tattnall, an officer whose scowling glance frightened all of his ship's young powdermonkeys.

The first week in April, a letter finally came, not from Eben's mother but from Becky Owens. With it in his hand, Eben went to find Jamie, who sat on the dock near the ship, fishing line in hand. Jamie looked up at Eben's call and asked, "What you got there? A letter, huh?"

"Uh-huh. What you got on your line, Jamie?"

"Nothing, not one bite yet."

"My letter's from Becky."

Jamie nodded. "What's she got to say for herself?"

"I dunno yet. I plan to read the letter to you. Here goes:

Dear Eben,

We were all glad to hear you are fine and were not hurt in that fight. Your ma is still a little mad at you, but she cries over you and that's a good sign. She is teaching me how to make a quilt and knit socks for soldiers.

Maybe it is a good thing that you cannot come home. Your mama wants her cousin who lives in the Blue Ridge Mountains to come with his wagon and take you home with him. That way, she says, you won't see any more water than there is in a little crick. Maybe she don't mean it, but I don't know about that.

Pa and Jason and your pa have not come yet. We don't get any letters from them, either. We hope they are all right and will miss them and pray for them. I am glad you and Jamie were heroes aboard the *Merrimack*. One of the reasons this letter comes so late is that I had to go back a couple of times to Jamie's house to find his mama at home and tell her that he is fine. She cried some, too.

Your friend, Becky Owens

P.S. Did you get the duds your ma sent you? She does not want you to go around dirty and shame her. I think she's proud of you like I am.

P.P.S. I can milk both of the cows now and do your other chores all right, but I do not take to the work.

Jamie had listened with care, and Eben noted how he'd whistled when he heard his mother had wept over him. When Eben finished reading, Jamie said, "Do tell! I'll take comfort from that, Eben."

"Are you gonna write her now?"

"Naw. If you write Becky again, tell her to tell my ma hello and that soon as I get paid, I'll send her some money." Jamie started to jiggle the fishing line and to hum "Aura Lee."

Eben knew by this that Jamie had said all he planned to say. How different this boy was from Jason, but how much he had come to like his former enemy! Someday maybe if it all worked out, the three of them could be friends together. Maybe they could be ship-mates on the same vessel and sail to China.

Lying at night in the powder magazine of his ship, Eben had made a deep decision. Trying to outrun the *Shrike* aboard the *Lucy,* then battling the *Cumberland* and *Congress* and *Monitor* just weeks ago had brought it about. He realized that the navy and a gunner's life penned up belowdecks were not for him. No, sir, he'd aim for a berth on a trading ship, one that carried cargoes, not cannon, and someday get his Master's papers to command his own ship on his own quarterdeck in the open air. The Lord willing, he'd ship out on the *Zephyr* if she made it through the war.

It was as clear and bright the morning of the eleventh of April as it had been in March when the *Merrimack* went out for the second time. Now Captain Tattnall decided he'd try the ship once more. Ready for combat with a new ram at her prow, the *Merrimack* steamed out of port into Norfolk Bay. The plan was to engage the *Monitor* in battle and at the same time have men from other Confederate ships board and take her. On his gun deck beside his cannon, Eben squatted excitedly at the gunport to see what he could. Where was the *Monitor?* Would she fight again?

He watched the wood-hulled blockaders sail swiftly out of the *Merrimack*'s way, and he heard a cheer from his crewmates who were watching from above. Then he saw her—lurking in the channel near Fortress Monroe. He shook his fists at her, making Kendrick shake his head. Would the *Monitor* come out? Would his ship go in after her?

Into late afternoon of that long day, Eben waited, wondering, torn between hope that they would fight, win, and break the blockade, and the fear of another dreaded cannon duel.

At four o'clock, the *Merrimack* fired three shots at the Yankee ironclad, but all fell short. At five, she steamed for port again.

The next day, she went out once more, but the Yankee ironclad kept her distance, unwilling to fight but yet protecting the other Union ships.

That night, Eben learned from Kendrick why their new captain had not gone in to attack the *Monitor*. Tattnall knew that the Yankee ironclad had hoped to lure the *Merrimack* deeper into the bay, where other Federal ships equipped with rams could smash into her hull to sink her.

More weeks went by with the blockade in full force. Then, on the eighth of May, Captain Tattnall took the *Merrimack* out once again. Hearing the Yankee ships firing on Sewell's Point, which was held by Confederate troops, he ordered his ship into the bay. Once more, Eben watched from his gunport. He saw all the Union ships withdraw, leaving the *Monitor* by herself in Hampton Roads. This time surely there would be a fight, he thought! He bit nervously at his nails, again hoping and fearing together. For two hours, however, the *Merrimack* only steamed about, cruising the Roads. Never did the *Monitor* come close enough so she could fire on her. The coward! Wary of other Yankee steamers and their rams, the *Merrimack* returned slowly to her anchorage, this time anchoring at Craney's Island. She had fired just one shot—but that was as a gesture of disgust at the cowardice of the *Monitor*'s captain.

Eben was in low spirits now, and not only because

the blockade stayed in force. The news about his home state of Virginia was not good. There was desperate trouble brewing. The Union general McClellan, a slow and cautious man, was massing an army to push into northern Virginia. His aim was surely to capture Richmond, and the capital of the Confederacy had to be defended by the South at all costs!

Norfolk, too, was threatened by the Yankees. Eben and his crewmates had been told that the city would soon be evacuated and abandoned to the Yankee bluebellies.

Eben worried about his mother and the Owens family. He asked Tom Kendrick, "What'll happen to Jamie's and my folks if the Yankees get hold of them?"

"Nothing much," the gunner replied, "if they don't give the Yankees any trouble. Bluebellies don't eat folks. It's our ship I'm most concerned about."

This made Eben scoff and say, "No Yankees can take the *Merrimack*."

"Probably not, but if they take Norfolk, the *Merrimack* won't have any port to go to even if she does bust the blockade. If she gets out to sea, she still has to have coal for her engines. You don't get coal out on the open sea. Besides, she ain't very seaworthy anyhow, remember? We're just going to have to sit here till we find out what Captain Tattnall has in mind to do next."

Eben now asked, "Can I send a letter to my ma?"

"Don't try it, lad. It wouldn't get delivered if the Yankees got hold of it."

What would the captain do? Eben went on wondering as the Confederates marched out on the tenth of May, setting fire to the Gosport Navy Yard before they left. The Yankees would be there almost at once and, as Kendrick had said, that meant the *Merrimack* would have no home port for repairs or supplies.

Eben and Jamie talked about the rumors they had heard that day. Some of the crew wanted to lighten the ship so she could steam up the rather shallow James River to Richmond and defend the city. Captain Tattnall, however, wanted to go out and attack the *Monitor* one last time. But could the Federal ironclad be taken? The thought of trying that again filled the two powderboys with fright and excitement.

The next day, an attempt was made to lighten the *Merrimack* by throwing overboard anything not absolutely needed, including food; but she could not be made light enough for the James. And the *Merrimack*'s pilots who knew the bay advised Captain Tattnall not to make the desperation attack against the *Monitor*.

In the end, the captain was forced to make a hard decision, one that dismayed his crew. When Eben heard what it was, he cried out in horror and knelt on the gun deck, battering it with his angry fists. Jamie wept outright, gulping in great sobs.

The *Merrimack,* their proud ship, was to be blown up by her own men!

The ironclad was run aground, and her crew, laden with food and pistols, went down her ladders for the last time. They were to march to Suffolk, a town some miles to the south, which was not yet taken by the Yankees.

Eben and Jamie stood together bidding farewell to their ship. They didn't speak. What could they say?

Marching with the others, Eben heard explosion after explosion coming from the northeast. He knew only too well what they were. The gunpowder charges placed aboard the *Merrimack* by Lieutenant Jones and his men had been ignited to set the wood hull on fire. His ship was now in flames!

CHAPTER ELEVEN

THE BLUFF AND THE ARMY

At five in the morning, as Eben and Jamie lay wrapped in blankets on a cobblestoned Suffolk street, the last great sound from the *Merrimack* came in a terrible roar that rattled windows in houses above the boys' heads. The fires set aboard her had reached her powder magazine. The Confederate ironclad was now truly gone.

Eben sat up with a crick in his back and sharp, stinging tears in his eyes. Infuriated at the injustice of this, he said, "It looks like what that old Yankee spy Jack Rawlins tried to do, Lieutenant Jones did better, huh, Jamie?"

Jamie answered with a sniffle, "It do look that way, don't it, Eben? What'll we do now without our ship?"

"Go where we're told to go, I guess. Nobody said to go home. And even if they did, how would we get past the Yankees?"

Gunner Kendrick went over to the boys not long after with bread, cheese, and coffee donated by Suffolk citizens. While they ate, he told them, "I just got our orders. The ship's officers are heading south to serve on other blockade runners down in Mobile, Alabama. We're going north toward Richmond—to a fort. It's on the James River on top of a high bluff."

Eben asked, "How come we're going there and not to another ship?"

"Because we think the *Monitor*'s aiming to go up that river headed to Richmond. They got some cannons at the fort, but they need cannoneers for them. We'll be doing on land what we did on water, but we'll be breathing in air instead of choking on gun smoke belowdecks."

Jamie laughed. "I sure ain't got no quarrel with that. Getting rid of that smoke would make me as happy as a hog in the sunshine."

Soon after, the officers of the *Merrimack* made their melancholy farewells to the crew and boarded a train headed south. Near noon, Eben, who felt sad at leaving his mother with nary a word, and Jamie clambered aboard flatcars that chugged north. Although they wondered whether they might be shot at by Yankee troops or encounter roving enemy cavalry, nothing happened. They were let off in the cool spring rain at the top of a cliff called Drewry's Bluff, overlooking the James River.

The two boys shared a hastily built hut with Gunner Kendrick and other men from their ship. Its roof leaked rainwater down onto Eben's head and shoulders as he tried to sleep. The food given them was poor—corn pone without molasses, fat salt pork, and little else. The local farmers sent their fresh meat and vegetables the seven miles to Richmond, where such things brought good prices.

Because of the heavy rains, the fort was a mire of mud. Each step Eben took almost pulled his boots from his feet. Disheartened by the destruction of his beloved ship and missing his comfortable dry bed in the powder magazine, he was miserable and irritable atop the cliff over the James. He thought much of his mother, worrying about her in the advance of the Union Army, but he couldn't be home to look after her and be here, too. His thoughts went also to his father and Captain Owens and Jason. Where were they? In France, or on the high seas sailing home while he trudged around in mud. And what would his father and the Owens men do when they learned Norfolk was in Yankee hands? Where would they go?

Two days of life at Drewry's Bluff brought Eben to

a peak of sour temper. He complained to Gunner Kendrick: "How do we know the Yankees'll come up the river to attack Richmond? How come we're still stuck here?"

Kendrick, who sat calmly and seemed oblivious to the rain, said, "We're here because that's where we got sent, Tyne. That's what happens in the navy. A man goes where he gets sent and does what he gets told."

Eben flared. "That don't mean I have to like it!"

"Me, neither," threw in Jamie.

The gunner said with a smile, "I don't like it, neither. I'd take the *Merrimack* over this anytime. I don't cotton to being a landlubber when I been a sailor so long. But this is where we got shipped. The Yankees'll come steaming up here with the *Monitor* sooner or later. We're here to give them a warm welcome from the Confederacy!"

Eben sulked. "I wish we could have blown that ship right out of the bay forever with our guns. I wish we'd blown every Yankee aboard her to kingdom come!"

"Do you, Tyne?" Tom Kendrick's voice was sharp. "You're pretty hot and quick to kill a lot of men, ain't you? They're people just like you and me—no better and probably not much worse, even if they are Yankees. Remember when our ship sank the *Cumberland*? There wasn't much cheering because our men knew there shouldn't be when other men had just got killed or maybe shot apart and would live maimed the rest of their lives." His eyes, fixed on Eben, hardened. "I told you before, Eben Tyne. You got too hot a temper for your own good. Do you know what your kind of temper does to a man's life?"

Eben stuck out his chin. "No, what does it do?"

"It gets him in trouble over and over again, and someday into more trouble than he can handle. You want to captain your own ship someday, don't you?"

"You know I do."

"Well, then, captain yourself first. The man who ain't got control of himself should never get the right to control other folks. I seen you shake your fists at the *Monitor* that one time, and I shook my head at you. Nobody on the *Monitor* could see you do that, so what good did it do? Get mad and show it and do something about it only if some good comes out of it and you're after good in the first place. Don't blow up like a cannon with a bad crew loading it. Think on it, boy."

With that, Gunner Kendrick strolled off to speak to Lieutenant Woods, a *Merrimack* officer still with them.

Jamie now turned to Eben to say, "He's right. You can get your dander up mighty easy, Eben. I do, too, but I got a reason. My ma don't fancy me much and nobody ever liked me at school the way they did you.

I ain't got a pa. You got one and a ma who dotes on you, and you ain't got a whole pack of brothers and sisters to have to share and fight with. Ain't nobody ever told you you fly off the handle sort of fast?"

Eben reddened and frowned. After a long while, he said, "Ma used to tell me so sometimes. I used to keep my hot feelings in around Pa, but not around her. She didn't like my getting mad easy. She said she thought I got that from her brother who got killed in a duel when he was twenty-two. She reckons his losing his temper got him shot dead."

Eben sighed deeply as he walked away to look down the bluff to the James River a hundred feet below. He'd try to think more about his temper from now on—"look before he leaped," as people said.

The morning of the fifteenth of May, Eben, Jamie, and the other *Merrimack* sailors were awakened by Lieutenant Woods's loud call. "Tumble out, you in there. The Yankees have come visiting us!"

It was six o'clock. During the night, the *Monitor* and another Union ironclad, the *Galena,* had led three wooden warships up to just below the bluff.

Pulling on his trousers, Eben stumbled to his gun while Jamie sprinted to his, pumping his heavy legs. It was battle stations all over gain, and once more it was the *Monitor!* Would she win this time? Or would they?

Eben's blood raced through his veins as it had when he carried powder to his cannon aboard the *Merrimack*. But this fight was different. He didn't run up and down into a dark hull for powder bags. Instead, he hurried into a clifftop shed, jostling other powderboys through a narrow door.

Shells and round shot hurtled down onto the enemy ships while the air on the cliff grew blue with powder smoke. This time, though, Eben could breathe through it, and his ears didn't hurt as they had inside the casement of the *Merrimack*.

He saw little of the battle save for his gun and its gun crew. Kept busy, it was some time before it came to him that there were no Yankee shells landing around him or sailing overhead, though he could hear their thudding from the river. Eben nodded grimly. He knew how the Yankee sailors were suffering. You bet he knew! Suddenly, he guessed what was happening. The ironclads and other Yankee ships below couldn't get their cannon to fire high enough to reach the top of Drewry's Bluff. All their shells fell short, embedding themselves in the cliff.

Despite this, the battle went on for four long hours with the Confederate cannon above firing down onto the *Monitor* and *Galena,* and the ironclads hammering the bluff while the wooden ships stayed out of Confederate range. Finally, however, the challenging ironclads withdrew downstream, with the other ships following them. A short cheer arose from the top of Drewry's Bluff. Richmond had been saved!

Shortly after the battle of the bluff, Eben and the other members of the *Merrimack*'s crew were sent to defend Richmond itself. Because the Yankees now realized they couldn't reach the capital city by water, they were coming by land.

As the boys walked north with the ironclad's crew, they saw signs of war wherever they looked. From time to time, Kendrick pointed out to them where houses had once stood and where crops had been burned or left untended, later to be beaten down by rain. There wasn't a cow or horse anywhere to be seen. Once, they passed by a wide meadow that had its grassy surface badly chewed up.

Tom Kendrick explained why. "There was a cavalry fight here," he said. "Look how the horses' hooves marked this up." He then pointed to white spots on the ground. "Those are bandages. It must have been a tough fight—fought with sabers, most likely. Saber cuts bleed bad. As for me, give me the big guns if I have to fight."

Turning to Eben, he asked, "Well, now that you've had yourself a taste of war, what do you think of it?"

Remembering his encounters with it—the *Lucy*'s and the *Merrimack*'s noise and searing smoke, his wounded knee, and his estrangement from his mother—Eben said truthfully, "I don't like it, Sir. A man would have to be crazy to!"

Kendrick laughed harshly. "Some men do. They love it! It makes them rich and it makes them famous, my curse to all of them!"

Before long, Richmond was in sight. The gun crews passed fighting trenches and the ruins of buildings that had been torn down to clear paths for cannon fire and to make room for maneuvering. The city was a fortress. Groups of soldiers and black slaves were busy setting up defenses to meet any attack of General McClellan's troops.

Eben marveled at the strange collection of arms in the hands of the Confederate soldiers he saw. They were of all types and sizes and lengths. Some were even ancient flintlocks. Scarcely anything was standard. Some troops were in uniform, while others wore whatever they had brought with them from home. Conflicting orders were being given to the men, who didn't know what they were supposed to be doing in the first place. This added to the noise and confusion. Surely there was some order here in Richmond, but it appeared to Eben that only the men in the rifle pits facing the enemy knew exactly what they were to do. Yet to a man they all seemed calm and reliant. He knew from the scrap at Drewry's Bluff that a Southern marksman could hit the head of a squirrel at fifty yards. Let the Yankee store clerks and factory workers come here and they would be dealt with!

As the *Merrimack* crew waited beside a cannon, talking with its crew of army gunners, a man in gray mounted on a coal-black horse came riding up. He called out, "I need cannoneers. Are there any men here who can join me?"

Quick as a flash, Gunner Kendrick ran up to him and said, "Aye, Sir, we're yours if you want us. We're off the ironclad."

"Yes. Too bad about your ship," said the Confederate cavalry officer. "I'd be Colonel Wade Hampton. Take two twelve-pounders from over there. Bring only two gun crews with you."

Eben knew he would be expected to go with Kendrick now to serve his master gunner's cannon. It was time for him and Jamie to split company. This had to be one of the worst things about war—first Jason, now Jamie going away. Eben went over to his friend and said, "I reckon this is good-bye for a while."

Jamie had heard everything, and said, "I reckon so, too, Eben. I'll go find my old gun captain now. Maybe we'll stay and defend the town."

"Maybe so, Jamie."

Their farewell was a far cry from the way they had acted as enemy schoolboys only months before. With a strong handshake and a muttered "Good luck, shipmate," Eben went back to his gunner.

• • •

Some three miles east of Richmond, the James River made a big bend in its course toward the sea. This was where Wade Hampton's Legion, nearly three hundred men and horses, rested under the trees awaiting orders. Army scouts were out combing the countryside for information. The news they brought their commander put his legion on the move again. Troop after troop filed by—in silence, as Hampton had commanded. Then the gunners were ordered to fall in, but without their powdermonkeys. Eben and the other boys who served the guns were to go to the rear of the column and help with the kitchen wagons, which were short of men. It was an odd order, but Eben hastened to obey.

From his position at the very end of the column, Eben could see the line of soldiers and horses weaving among the trees, with the sunlight glistening now and then on the barrels of the cannon. He saw tall Tom Kendrick beside his gun and wished he was with him. Kitchen work was not for him!

Hours passed as Eben walked with his handkerchief to his nose to keep out the dust kicked up by the horses. He missed the crisp, fresh-smelling, salt-laden sea air he'd known all his life. He was a seafarer, not a landsman.

Beside him walked another one-time powderboy, a lanky fair-haired lad from Newport News named

Billy Ashe. Billy wasn't looking forward to scouring pots, either.

At dusk, the cook called out that they would stop and make a trail dinner for the cavalrymen. Eben didn't know what a trail dinner might be and so he asked the old cook.

"That'd be the flattest johnnycake you'll ever see, navy boy; jest meal, lard, water, and salt, with coffee and beans. That's what cavalry gits on campaigns. When we pull up a bit, they gits fried taters, beans, and steak." He ordered, "Hop to it, you boys. We be needing wood for fires. Them troops will be crazy hungry. When they get here, we'll be right popular for a spell!" After he spat a wad of tobacco juice to knock a fly off the tail of the wheel horse, he added, "That horse has got the cleanest hind end in all Virginny."

As Eben and Billy walked away to gather firewood, Eben looked back at the cook. Truly, he was an uncommonly accurate spitter. The boys were still grinning at the cook's amusing antics as they looked for fallen branches in the woods. Talking softly, they moved out of sight of the cook wagon into a stand of trees a distance away.

The jingle of metal brought Eben to a sudden halt, his arms filled with wood. Hampton's men were ahead of him, moving quietly as ordered on the trail, so who was making all this noise of harness and bridle jinglings?

Holy crow, these must be Yankees!

Shouting *"Yankees! Clear out!"* to Billy, Eben dropped the wood he had collected and sprinted toward the wagon, where he knew the old cook kept a rifle under the seat.

With both his heart and feet pounding furiously, Eben ran as hard as he could. He wasn't any match for the horse pursuing him, however. A rawboned roan tossed its foamy mouth in his face as a blue-uniformed trooper pulled it to a sliding stop. With four hooves planted in the sod, the horse had its nose only inches from Eben's nose.

From the top of the horse, a soft Irish voice said, "Easy there, me lad. Don't ye make me do it. Stand easy!"

Eben was looking into the muzzle of a huge horse pistol. Death swifter and surer than the bite of a copperhead snake was there. The boy lifted his eyes to the broad red face over him. "I give up, Sir."

"All right, slowly now, laddie-buck. Back to the wagon" came the command. "You hold tight to me stirrup. If ye don't, ye jest might get shot."

A prisoner! He was a Yankee captive of war. Red rage rather than fear filled his being. Eben wanted to shriek with fury and disappointment, but he held the cry as an ache in his throat. It wouldn't befit a powderboy off the *Merrimack,* nor a son of Captain Sam Tyne, to do that.

The Yankee cavalry patrol had run across the Confederate cavalry's supply wagon. As Eben looked on, the Federals rounded up the seven men who made up the kitchen detail. He saw that somehow Billy Ashe had made his escape and, though he felt his own sorrow deeply, he rejoiced for him.

Now there came a popping like the firecrackers Captain Walter had once brought back from a China voyage on the *Zephyr* and sold in Norfolk. The sound came from the woods in front of Eben. It was rifle fire! Hampton's troopers were fighting the enemy cavalry. However, that meant they couldn't come to his rescue, and a prisoner he was to remain.

His march to the Union encampment was a short one because the Yankees were situated on the same ridge the Confederates had hoped to camp on. A collision was inevitable, and now it had taken place.

A small, fluttering red and white swallow-tailed flag, its pole stuck in the ground, marked the headquarters of the Third Squadron, 6th United States Cavalry. Below it was a tan-colored canvas awning, and under it sat a tall Yankee officer.

One after the other, the Confederate prisoners were brought before him and asked their names and their units. Answers varied greatly as each man invented army outfits that had never existed, hoping to throw him off. Eben's turn before the officer came last of all.

"I want your name and outfit so we can tell your side that we're holding you prisoner and that you aren't wounded."

Eben told the truth. Why not? He had no ship anymore. "Eben Tyne, Sir. Powdermonkey off the *Merrimack*, the C.S.S. *Virginia*."

The major's brows raised. He said, "Navy, you say? That's hard to believe, but a lot of things in war are. You don't wear Confederate gray." After noting on a piece of paper what Eben had said, he waved the boy aside.

Then the Union officer stood up and, looking at the captives, said, "Big as Hampton's Legion is, isn't it odd that never a man is ever captured from it! You're a bunch of liars. I know who you are. You're all going to the stockade, and I promise you that you will not like it there."

Marching under the rifles of five all-too-alert guards, the unhappy, resentful captives slogged without rest miles down a road to the rear of the Union forces. In six hours' time, they arrived at the Wakerton Farm. It was already dark, and they were tired and hungry. The guards found places for them to rest in an empty supply wagon, but there were neither blankets nor food for the men. They were left to lie down on the wagon bed to sleep as best they could.

· CHAPTER TWELVE ·

PRISONERS

Eben fell asleep from exhaustion. It had been an evil day, the worst in his life.

He didn't fully realize he was a prisoner until he awakened at daybreak, shivering, hungry, and scared. Then the impact of what had happened to him hit as he saw his prison for the first time.

The stockade, just outside the village of Tappahannock, was only a stock-fence enclosure that was set smack-dab in the middle of a big open field. At first, it didn't look too bad to him. When they were herded into the stockade at gunpoint, Eben saw there was a small stream meandering through it, and there didn't seem to be too many prisoners. The big surprise came when he looked from the heavy gates of the prison and saw that it had only three sides. The fourth was just one single deep furrow in the sod.

Seeing the surprise on Eben's and several other faces, the guard nearest to him told them, "That's the dead man's line! Cross it even by accident and we'll shoot you. We shoot to kill. We haven't got medicine here to doctor wounds, so a wound means gangrene and a hard way to die. You Johnny Rebs just stay this side of that line and you'll live." The Yankee added, "You'll be getting food in the morning and the evening. You can get your water from the crick. You're free to go anywhere that suits you here, but remember that dead man's line." Now he shifted his rifle to a more comfortable position, spat on the ground, turned, and walked away.

Hampton's kitchen detail, including Eben, explored the enclosure in a body. One of the captured men, a young black-haired soldier not much older than Eben, drawled in disgust, "They ain't gonna keep me in here. No Yankee's going to hold me. Soon as it gets dark, I'm running for it over that line of theirs and into the trees, where they ain't never going to find me." He looked from face to face, grinning. Then he spoke directly to Eben. "How about you, boy? You're off the *Merrimack,* ain't you? That means you got some grit. Was you at that scrap with the Yankee ironclad?"

"Yes, I was there," Eben said proudly.

The soldier nodded. "Well, that wasn't no lemonade sociable for young ladies, was it? Have you got the sand in your craw to make a run for it with me tonight?"

Eben looked behind him at the dead man's line and the patrolling sentry. No Yankee stockade was going to keep him a prisoner. Anger he had held in check flooded his soul now. Why not wait till dark and run with this soldier?

"Sure, I'll go with you."

An older soldier advised, "That's crazy talk, you two. Let's build a brush lean-to in the corner of this stockade and wait and see what'll happen."

"What can happen?" demanded the young soldier angrily.

"Our cavalry can ride in and save us."

The black-haired youth spat at the man's feet. "They should have done that when we was being marched along before we got here. That was the time for it. There're too many bluebellies here to try anything against this place. I'll help you make a lean-to, but I don't aim to sleep in it. Me and this *Merrimack* boy'll get free and find lots of cavalry to ride down on this place, set you all free, and burn it."

"You're a tomfool, Ezra," said a red-bearded prisoner. He turned to Eben. "You're a fool, too, son, if you go with him."

Eben flared. "I can make up my own mind for my-self!"

"Suit yerself, kid."

Angry at the interference, Eben stalked off to sit alone and brood, his knees pulled up to his chest. He looked across the way. The black-haired soldier was helping construct the lean-to. His face was like a thunderhead.

Eben sat motionless for hours, thinking, thinking.

His thoughts turned again and again to his father and mother and to the older Owenses. But, as dusk came on, he thought now mostly of Becky and Jason. What would they do if they could see his plight right now? He thought hard and deeply, harder than he had ever done in his life. Yes, they would say to him, "Stay put, Eben, and come home to us alive. Don't try to escape tonight." That's just what they would say. They wouldn't want him to risk his life.

After all the thinking he had been doing, the anger began to fade, until only sadness remained. The fury had buoyed him and now it was gone, but he didn't mourn its passage. It had been a moment's silly rage at the man who had called him a fool that had made it blaze up so.

Eben made up his mind. He put away the anger that could get him killed tonight. He stared at the black-haired soldier, who was stalking back and forth now like an animal. The soldier looked crazy. Once, he had stopped pacing and glared at Eben. His burning eyes made Eben shudder.

No, he would do best to stay here a prisoner and wait and see how things turned out. Maybe his mother had had to leave their house, and maybe his pa was in trouble, too. Did he have to add to their woes?

When it was full dark and camp fires were blazing, Eben arose and walked stiffly over to the black-haired soldier, who sat alone.

Eben told him, "I been thinking, and I think it'd be better if I didn't try to run and better if you didn't, either. Don't you have any folks who'd care?"

"Sure I do. That's why I'm going—to see them soon again." The soldier looked up at Eben with contempt, his face scowling in the red firelight. "I don't want to be in any bluebelly prison camp the rest of the war. Who knows how long that'll last? Maybe they exchange prisoners—Yankees for Confederates—but you can't count on that. You got a lily liver, boy. I bet you hid in the bottom of the *Merrimack* crying for your ma when your ship went out to fight. I think you're a mawmouth."

Two months past, Eben would have flung himself onto the soldier, even though this man was larger and older. Then he would have hit him hard as he could. Not now, though, not after living with the thoughts he had had all day. Eben sighed, said, "Good luck to you," and went to sit at one of the camp fires where Hampton's kitchen detail were squatting on the grass.

The bearded man asked him quietly, "Are you going with that hothead over there?"

"No, sir, I'm not. I decided against it. Being foolish don't mean being brave."

"Good for you, lad," said the man.

Near midnight, the camp was roused by a rattling of shots, scarlet flashings, and a scream. Without having to be told, Eben knew that the young soldier had made his break for freedom and had gotten only a few feet over the dead man's line before he was shot dead. He saw his sprawled body in the morning, the brown eyes open to the sky, before the Yankees hauled him away by his legs to bury him.

The bearded soldier beside Eben said, "He never did sleep in our lean-to, did he? Ain't you glad you did?"

"Yes, sir."

That morning, the prisoners learned what their captors had in mind for them. After a breakfast of grits and water, they were formed into ranks and sent out under heavy guard to fell timbers to make up the fourth wall of the hastily erected stockade.

Eben's work was different. He and the other captured boys were ordered to peel bark off the poles.

This was labor he quickly came to hate, as splinters drove themselves cruelly into his palms and fingers. At sunset, he was exhausted not only from peeling bark but from helping to haul back to camp the thirty poles that had been cut and stripped. Though the Yankees had horses, they forced the prisoners to do this.

Aching in his back, arm, and hands, Eben had never been so weary before—not even after the battles aboard the *Merrimack*. He wanted only to sink down onto the grass and rest. He took no interest in the news that more Confederate captives had been brought in while he was out peeling logs in the forest.

Wrapped in a blanket a Yankee guard had thrown to him, Eben sat head downward against the stockade until he heard a voice he knew. "Well, Eben Tyne, here we be together again, eh?"

Tom Kendrick!

Eben flung back his head. It *was* his gunner. He looked bad—worse than Eben had ever seen him— as if somebody's dog had gotten him under a house. He was gray and tattered and wearing the start of a beard. How had the bluebellies ever gotten hold of him?

Kendrick eased himself to the ground. As if he had guessed Eben's question, he said, "The outfit I was in got ambushed by Yankee troops inside some deep woods. Our cavalry rode off, wanting to regroup and attack the bluebellies, so they left us. We couldn't follow them and dodge trees and go down ravines—not with cannons, we couldn't. So I got taken prisoner with my cannon, and I got marched here by the bluebelly cavalry." He took a deep breath and added, "We've got poor luck, Tyne, it appears to me. First we lose our ship and now the army's gun. What'll come next, the good Lord only knows!"

Now Eben quietly told him of the black-haired soldier and his own decision not to try to escape with him.

Kendrick nodded. "You did right. I'm proud of you. I'd say you captained yourself."

Eben sighed and said mournfully, "Thank you, Mr. Kendrick. I surely do miss our ship."

"So do I, so do I. A man can lose a lot he values in a war, and not just his life."

Eben asked, "Did you tell the bluebellies you were with Wade Hampton or off our ship? I told them I was off the *Merrimack*."

The gunner laughed. "I said I was off the *Merrimack*, too. I don't think they believed me, though. They don't expect to find sailors in the cavalry."

Cutting logs, dragging them back, digging postholes, and building the fourth side of the stockade kept the prisoners busy as the days went by. Each day seemed longer than the one before to Eben, even with his shipmate beside him now. Though weary from hard labor and the monotony of their work routine, what tormented Eben the most was the complete absence of any war news. No guard ever told them a single word of what went on in the state. If Richmond had fallen to the Yankees, they didn't get the word. And what was going on with his mother and the Owens family? Were they hungry? Had their gardens done well enough this year to feed them? There had been a lot of rain, maybe too much. Did his mother know that he, Eben, was a captive? Or did she think he was dead because she didn't hear from him? Did that Yankee officer really let her know what had happened to him? Eben had little faith that his fate was known to her.

Eben kept reliving his last meeting with his mother in his mind. He'd done his duty by the *Merrimack,* but in doing that, how he'd hurt her! Had Pa come home yet, and Mr. Owens and Jason? Could they even get to Norfolk now that the Yankees held it? Where was Jamie Sloat—a prisoner in yet another log stockade?

One day ten long days after Tom Kendrick had come to join him, Eben and he were sitting on a log at their corner of the stockade, now called Camp Sparks. A guard came up to the two of them and ordered them to report at once to the camp commander. Neither had ever been called to him before. Eben looked at the gunner with fright.

Kendrick told him, "No, I don't know what this is about, either, but we better take our bedrolls with us—just in case."

Eben protested. "We haven't done anything wrong. Nobody else here has ever been called to him."

"Aye, it's odd, but let's go, Eben. We've got no choice."

A startling surprise greeted them as they entered the little wood and canvas office of Captain Sparks, who looked at them, grunted, and ordered, "Turn around, you sailors!"

Eben and the gunner turned as ordered, and both gasped in amazement. There stood Jack Rawlins, Commander Rawlins of the United States Navy, in a blue Union uniform. The right sleeve of his officer's coat had been doubled over and pinned to his shoulder. He had only one arm now.

The master gunner spoke first. "Well, I guess I should have known this all along. Even in Tripoli, when you stood a hard life with your shipmates, you were really a Yankee officer all along. What you did aboard the *Merrimack* all fits together now."

"Aye, Tom Kendrick. We were good shipmates once, but the needs of the Union came first. I chose to serve the North and its cause. I had a job to do aboard the *Merrimack,* just like you did. It wasn't the kind of work I like to do. I don't fancy spy work. It's a dirty trade. I've come here to say to you and the boy that there's still a job for you two, if you will take it. I can use you! That's why I had you two called out when I got the reports that two people I might know from the *Merrimack* were here in this camp."

He looked at Eben, his pale eyes gleaming and his voice soft as he said, "I bet you have some questions for me. You generally did. Let's have them, laddie."

Eben said severely, "You pretended to be my friend, yet you tried to blow up our ship! I saw you at it. So did my friend Jamie Sloat. But we beat you. We bit through the fuses you lit to stop you. We were in the powder magazine the night you and the others came."

Rawlins smiled. "So that's why the charges failed to blow, huh! You two bit through them! Well, that's remarkable. I never knew you boys were in the magazine. I *am* your friend. I respect you as a Confederate Navy powderboy. Nothing has changed that. Yes, I did try to destroy your ship, but my reason for doing that was to save lives—not to take them. Your ship was doomed from the very start."

Seeing the smoldering anger in Eben's and Kendrick's eyes, Rawlins went on: "She was far too slow and couldn't maneuver well. She was made up of worn-out parts. Yes, she could have won her fights in the harbor, but soon more of our own ironclads would come to fight her. Valiant as her crew was, she'd eventually lose a fight because of her bad engines. Many men would die aboard her. I don't like to see men die. My duty to the Union came first. I make no apology to you."

Eben stood mute, his emotions mixed. What Commander Rawlins had said about the *Merrimack* was true, but to admit it was a different thing. Yes, her crew had done nothing but make repairs. With decent engines, the *Merrimack* would have been invincible in calm waters, but there were no new ship's engines in the South, only in the North. What her crew had had was valor aplenty, but what was that pitted against new and trustworthy equipment in the long run?

He heard Mr. Kendrick speaking to Rawlins. "It appears you were badly used somewhere, Jack!" He pointed to the empty sleeve.

"Yes, I was aboard the *Cumberland* when she came up against the *Merrimack* in March. Perhaps your gun did this to me, who knows? I'm glad to see that you two made it away onto land without any souvenirs like mine. But I'm not here at a prison camp to talk of my wound. I've come on something more important. Captain Sparks"—he spoke to the burly camp commander—"I want these two prisoners of war paroled to me at once. I know them, as you can see. I believe I can rely on the honor of their given word to you. I want to take them with me for about seven hours. Tom, do you give me your solemn word not to try to escape if I don't ask Captain Sparks here for guards?"

"Aye, Jack. You have my word—for seven hours, but not for more."

"And, Eben Tyne, what about you?"

"Aye, Sir, same as my gunner."

"Good. Captain Sparks, we won't need your guards. Thank you. I see these men have their bedrolls. Take them back. They won't be needing them, I think. Now I'll sign the sheet that gives the responsibility for these two rebel prisoners to me."

As Eben and Kendrick deposited their bedrolls outside the door, Eben wondered about the seven hours of liberty they were granted. Where were they going? And why?

Stepping out the door to join his former shipmates of the *Merrimack,* Jack Rawlins told them, "Gunner Kendrick, Powderboy Tyne, you are paroled to me. Get in that carriage." He pointed at a four-horse buggy that was just pulling up to the door.

The two ragged and dirty Confederates obeyed. They were promptly joined by the commander, who ordered the driver to proceed. With the sleek bays trotting swiftly, the carriage moved northward.

Rawlins commanded sharply now, "Ask me no questions right now. Check the basket under your seat, young Tyne. I think you might find something in it worthwhile."

With a little tug, Eben hauled a wicker basket up onto the seat. He opened it and looked up in joyful amazement. Cooked mashed corn and golden brown fried chicken were settled in the bottom of the basket, along with sourdough biscuits and country pickles. Even a small jug of corn whiskey peeked its neck up in the corner. Two small glasses stood beside it.

Seeing Kendrick's eyes rest on the crockery jug, Jack Rawlins told him, "This is for old times, shipmate Kendrick. You and I will drink to them. Please pull the cork and fix the glasses. I cannot do that with only one hand, you see." Again Eben heard the steel voice of authority cloaked in courtesy.

"Aye, Sir. It will be but a minute." Eben watched the gunner uncork the bottle and fill the glasses. "To old times, Sir!" Kendrick toasted, raising his glass, addressing the commander.

"And to those perhaps yet to come" was the mysterious reply from Rawlins.

The fine carriage traveled smoothly on the graded dirt road. The chicken, the corn, and biscuits disappeared. As Eben ate the last pickle, Jack Rawlins came to the business at hand. "There are three things I am taking you both to see. The first of them is around that bend in the road ahead of us."

Eben looked ahead but saw nothing unusual,

though he heard a dull roaring sound. As the carriage covered the distance to the wide bend, hundreds of tents came into view. Dust rose from the boots of thousands of men in blue uniforms, drilling in formation, battalion upon battalion. Apart from the massed men, Union cavalry and horse artillery charged and countermarched in make-believe attacks up each side of the enormous field. Bugle calls rang out over and over again.

The Yankee told them dryly, "That's only one brigade you see here. New ones are being raised in the North every day. The Union has no shortage of men as the South has." He stopped, allowing the two prisoners a chance to gauge the Yankee might.

Now the horses went on again. The miles sped by to the regular drum of hooves. As they rode, the abundance of the North sank slowly into Eben's unwilling consciousness. Yes, even though the men of the South had more spirit and were better marksmen, the Yankees had horses and men to spare. Soon it would come down to a dozen Yankees against one Confederate, and a better-equipped Yankee, too. They had well-made, warm uniforms, and they probably had a lot of food. Even the horses trotting in front of him were well filled out and strong-looking.

Deep in thought, Eben raised his head and saw they had come to a bridge and were to cross the headwaters of a little bay. As the carriage swept past the Yankee guards and onto the planks of the bridge, Commander Rawlins, as if he knew what Eben was staring at, motioned to a mass of boxes, bales, and sacks on the shore of the bay just over the bridge.

Rawlins told him, "Go ahead. Get out and take a look."

The words were barely out of his mouth when the carriage stopped, and both Kendrick and Eben climbed down. What awaited Eben's inspection shocked him. Crate after wooden crate stood piled in rows taller than the gunner. Some were marked with black-painted stencils—RIFLES, REMINGTON CAL. .50—while others bore markings identifying cases of pistols, boxes of cartridges, and barrels of cannon powder. To the right of Eben was a series of wooden frames. Atop these pallets neatly aligned, their bores pointing toward the bay, stood row after row of twelve-pounder field-artillery cannon, powerful guns to be turned on the Confederacy, and at that very moment pointing south toward her.

Eben saw piles of saddles, boxes of sabers, stacks of horse harnesses, and small mountains of cloth sacks. Going over to one and opening it, he saw it was filled with wheat. Another was full of dried beans. Others had been packed with coffee and tobacco. Off to one side of these were ambulance wagons—under his breath Eben counted seventeen—and alongside them, a small hill of medical supplies.

As Eben and Kendrick completed their inspection, they came to stand facing one another, speechless. Kendrick shook his head sadly.

Getting back into the carriage, Eben and his gunner had nothing to say. Rawlins remarked simply, "This is a supply depot. There are many like it that will furnish our troops with whatever they need. This depot," he went on, "is the second thing I wanted you to see. Eben, you don't know me as well as Tom Kendrick does. He'll tell you I may act a part, but I don't lie. What you have just seen is only a small part of the North's power. There is much more nearby. Seven hours' leave won't let us see all of it by a long shot. Tom is older and wiser than you, Eben, so I doubt if I need to ask him what the outcome of this war is going to be. I can see by his face that I don't have to. But what about you, young Tyne?"

"I believe you, Sir, but what we're going to do is go on fighting you Yankees all the same. I know that!"

"So do I, but I wanted you two to see what the South is going to have to face from now on. She will go on as long as she can fight. I know how strong-willed Confederates are. After all, I'm a Marylander, myself." He went on, looking suddenly melancholy. "But each day the South goes on fighting, it will be more costly to her than the day before, and we Union men can't do a thing about it but go on fighting, too.

You won't give up slavery to rejoin the Union, and we won't let you destroy that."

Kendrick asked sullenly, "Aren't our seven hours about up?"

"Not quite, according to my watch. It's time you see the third and last thing I have in mind to show you. It's nearby. Driver, go to dock number seven."

The glossy bays trotted along the front of the supply depot to where the harbor opened up before them. They were on the bay at the mouth of the Rappahannock River. How sweet the sea air smelled, and Eben breathed it in deeply, filling his lungs. Next to the sea, he loved the docks best.

Near the side of the dock was a trim little brig. Eben looked at her appreciatively. She would be fast, he knew, and could take any ocean winds she might meet. The Yankee flag flew at her stern.

Eben's and Kendrick's curious eyes went to Rawlins, who was clearly enjoying his moment of suspense. He said matter of factly, "She's the *Eaglet,* United States Navy brig, carrying six guns, John Rawlins commanding."

Astonishment came over Eben's face. A one-armed man commanding a ship of war? Such things didn't happen.

Seeing Eben glance at his empty sleeve, the Yankee officer explained. "After I lost my arm, they wanted to put me on the beach at a desk. I called in some favors due me from the navy for my actions in Tripoli, and the navy listened. I have a special assignment now. I can pick my own crew. They are on board at this very moment. I need cannoneers, and I ask you two to join the ship." He paused, then added, "But perhaps you'd rather go back and cut more logs at Camp Sparks?"

Eben couldn't believe his ears. Betray the South?

Rawlins ignored the stunned and resentful silence from the man and boy, and motioned for them to come aboard his ship. He continued talking from her deck. "As I said, I have a special assignment." He gazed up into the taut rigging of the *Eaglet*. "This ship will never fire on your Confederate flag. I promise you that in full faith. Her post is to be in the Caribbean. With the war going on in America, all control's been lost down there. Piracy will start up again, and the *Eaglet*'s job will be to put a stop to that. Oh, there could be fighting and plenty of it." Now, using the nautical terms of a hundred years past, he challenged them with, "Be ye two seamen with me and with my ship, sailing under the Union flag, for the only purpose I stated to ye?"

"Aye, Sir," answered Tom Kendrick with no hesitation. "Aye, to fighting pirates."

"Then, Master Gunner Kendrick, look at your guns, they lay forward to your quarters. You'll find all you need there."

Touching his head in a salute, Kendrick moved off to inspect his new ship.

Left alone, feeling deserted, Eben found himself asked sharply, "What about you, Tyne?"

The boy waited, scowling, considering, while Rawlins told him, "Listen well. We could be together a long time. I'll send a letter to your home in Norfolk telling your people about you. There are ways to get a note to them even if they are known Confederates. How it gets to them doesn't matter, but I assure it will get there. It will say that you are well and that you are going out with me on a ship that is forbidden to fight Confederate vessels of war or merchant ships, only pirates."

While Rawlins spoke to him, Eben had been looking past him to watch Kendrick's departure. He was filled with horror and disgust. His gunner a traitor to the South, a turncoat! Hot anger half-choked him. Let him go. Let Tom go. Be damned to him! Log cutting for Yankee soldiers was better than this. No! Captain Tyne's son would stay true to the Stars and Bars, no matter how many logs he'd have to peel at Camp Sparks.

Camp Sparks! Eben's work-roughened hand went now to his mouth as the sea breeze ruffled his over-long hair. Wait! It wasn't one bit like Tom Kendrick to make a decision against the Confederacy, and to make it this swiftly was beyond belief. Why had he done it? Think, Eben, think! It must have to do with fighting pirates. Kendrick had gone to sea for years. He had been at Tripoli in the Mediterranean Sea. There were pirates in those waters. He would know about pirates, then. He would know more than Eben Tyne would.

Eben's eyes went to Rawlins now. He asked, "Do you think I'd ever fight for the North? Aren't the pirates in the Caribbean helping the South by coming out to take your Yankee ships?"

Rawlins shook his head. "You don't know pirates, my boy. They don't care what ship they take and plunder. They'll take Confederate vessels in a minute, too. There'll be pirates waiting for us in the West Indies. They're the devils of the sea. They're devils on land, too. They fight sometimes on land, you know. Soldiers from an army will take a town and subdue it and maybe burn it, but they don't murder every man, woman, and child in it. Pirates do! They don't leave anything alive behind them. They don't know any military laws. They're blood-mad murderers. I can smell them sea miles away, and so can Tom Kendrick. We'll be seeing action against *pirates!*"

Eben paused, thinking, letting the powerful words sink in.

Rawlins went on. "I think you might be interested to know that your father and some men named Owens returned two weeks ago from France. They did not get what they went after, but they are not prisoners of war because they are still civilians. Your mother is well."

Eben drew in his breath. With his eyes on Kendrick, who was now standing at a cannon a distance away, he said slowly, "I reckon I could serve under you as a powdermonkey, but I won't ever turn into a Yankee. Never will I do that!"

"Nobody is asking you to do that, Tyne. All right, I will send the letter I spoke to you about just now." Commander Rawlins went to lean on the rail to look down into the still waters of the harbor, then said softly, "We won't talk like this again, but hear me now. Your world is open to you. Because you were only a powderboy for the Confederacy, you can still become an officer in the U.S. Navy someday. I wish it was the same with Gunner Kendrick, for no better man do I know. But he can never be an officer in our navy; they'll never let him."

After he'd drawn a deep breath, Eben told Rawlins boldly, "Sir, I don't think I really want to serve all my life in the navy. I want to be a master of a merchantman that goes all over the world for cargoes."

"That's a fine ambition, too. Now off you go to your quarters with the gun crews. There's a seaman's kit ready for you."

Eben saluted his captain and turned smartly around

to go belowdecks. In turn, Commander Rawlins took two envelopes from his pocket and handed them to a sailor standing nearby, waiting—letters to the Tynes and to the commandant of Camp Sparks. Then the Yankee commander turned to watch Eben walking toward Kendrick, who now waited at the top of the companionway leading to the crew's quarters. Rawlins sighed, then smiled as Gunner Kendrick stood looking down into Eben's face. The grinning master gunner put his hand on the boy's shoulder and said, "I'm glad you decided to ship aboard."

Eben asked, "Are you sure we're doing the right thing in fighting for the Yankee navy?"

"I do when it comes to fighting pirates. No American who can fight at all should let pirates live."

Eben thought for a long moment, then said, "I reckon that Americans, wherever they were born, are all the same to pirates. They're everybody's enemy. I suppose we can be Americans first of all when it comes to pirates and be Southerners second. That idea runs on all fours with me. It doesn't mean I have to turn into a Yankee, though, and neither do you."

"I don't intend to," said Kendrick.

Now both of them fell silent as they heard the rattling noises of the gangplank being brought on board and Commander Rawlins's voice giving orders to his officer of the deck. "Mr. Paul, let go fore and aft. Bend on topsails and topgallants. Head her for Jamaican waters."

"Aye, Sir, Jamaican waters it be!" came the ringing reply that held both joy and defiance in it.

"Holy crow! Pirates!" exclaimed Eben Tyne aloud.

And then he laughed.

AUTHORS' NOTE

Eben Tyne, Powdermonkey has been written to show today's young reader the far too infrequently presented part taken by the South in a single, very significant engagement of the American Civil War. This engagement emphasized the belief of the South that its valor, its dedication to The Cause, and its willingness to sacrifice would overcome the industrial might of the North. To an extent, this belief held true, especially during the time frame of this book. A small force from the Confederacy had routed a much larger Union one at the Battle of Bull Run. The North had surrendered Fort Sumter in Charleston harbor, thus removing the threat of seaborne invasion from there. At this time, the South looked hopefully to either England or France for support in its fight for independence.

The South had bountiful supplies of cotton and, to a lesser degree, tobacco, which were in demand in Europe. For the most part, the sparsely settled agricultural South based its economy on these crops. Most of the people who lived there were close to the soil. They were often expert woodsmen and riflemen. By and large, the rural Southerner was self-sufficient, proud, and quick to protect his honor. To his way of thinking, the North was populated by factory workers, poor-spirited drones who took orders and pulled levers on machinery—certainly not fighting men. "Any Southerner is worth ten Yankees in a scrap" was the common belief.

The events leading to the 1862 battle between the C.S.S. *Virginia* (called the *Merrimack* in this book for simplicity's sake) and the U.S.S. *Monitor* came at a time when the South enjoyed the military edge on the land. While Yankee commanders arranged their forces in set positions to fight when they felt the time was right, the South maneuvered freely to strike at will. At sea, however, it was different. President Lincoln had swiftly ordered blockades of the Southern ports. His Union Navy (which consisted of only 5 percent of Northern forces at any time) kept most of the Confederate shipping bottled up. The cotton the South could have sold to buy guns, medicines, and machinery was piled up on the wharves, useless. Desperate for sailors, the South took them out of army regiments.

Though she would not have been seaworthy enough to break blockades up and down the whole Southern coast, the *Merrimack* was the only ship that could break the Norfolk blockade. Had the U.S.S. *Monitor* delayed her arrival by even a day, Norfolk's waters could have been cleared and Southern ships could have sailed in and out until the Union land forces sealed the city some months later.

The chief importance of that small naval battle starting on the eighth of March 1862 and ending on the ninth was that it changed the conduct of naval battles and strategy forever. The era of the wooden warship was at an end; that of the ironclad warship had begun.

In this novel, we have written of the end of the *Merrimack*. Her life was a brief one. So was that of the *Monitor*. She sank in a gale December 31, 1862, fifteen miles off Cape Hatteras, North Carolina. Sixteen members of her crew went to the bottom with her. In 1974, the wreck was located and photographed by divers in 220 feet of water. Today, people are interested in raising the *Monitor* or parts of her to study our heritage and to serve as a type of maritime museum. Raising her could prove very expensive, however, and may eventually even require the aid of America's schoolchildren, as the refitting of the U.S.S. *Constitution*—our revered "Old Ironsides"—did in the 1930s.

The battle between the two ironclads is presented here as it actually took place; so is the previous day's fight with the wood-hulled ships. McClellan's army on the peninsula, the defense of Richmond, and the very rapid buildup of Union military strength are historically correct, as is the account of the brief battle of Drewry's Bluff in May of 1862.

The ships mentioned in the early part of this book, the *Lucy* and *Zephyr,* are fictional, as is the U.S.S. *Shrike.* Navy ships facing the *Merrimack,* however, are real vessels.

A number of people of whom we write are actual individuals in history. Wade Hampton, Lieutenant Catesby R. ap Jones, Captain Franklin Buchanan, Mr. John M. Brooke, and Captain Josiah Tattnall each filled the same role he has in *Eben Tyne, Powdermonkey.* Eben, Jason, Jamie, Tom Kendrick, Commander Rawlins, and the Tyne and Owens families are the creations of the authors. These characters aren't intended to represent any particular individual of that era, although collectively they can be said to represent the many supporters who rallied to the Stars and Bars of the Confederacy not because they adhered to slavery but because they supported states' rights over the

Union. Some people believed that the individual status of their state was more important than that of the Federal government. They held that a state should not have to conform to everything the U.S. Congress laid down as law.

Today's young readers may be surprised and dismayed at what seems harshness on the part of parents and other adults toward the child characters in this story. Children were by no means as protected as they are today, even in a one-child family. Though that did not mean they were less loved, a child was expected to grow up much faster then. *Teenager* is a word of quite recent vintage. A thirteen-year-old was expected to conduct himself or herself as a responsible adult—to do an adult's work around a ship, a farm, or a house. Most children left school at twelve and received no further education. The word of the father was usually law to everyone, including his wife. There were many boy runaways in the last century. If a boy refused to obey his parents, running off was his way of escape. Both the grandfather and the father of the authors did exactly that. There were no child-centered courts of law or caring social workers to look after him. Had Eben or Jason refused the duty for the Confederacy their fathers chose for them, they would have shamed the men, who could have disowned them. For a sizable lad of twelve to fourteen to fill a man's post in the army or navy was not so rare then. In some army regiments, the drummer boys were only ten years old and expected to go into battle—and they did.

To the best of our knowledge, no blacks ever served on the crews of either the *Merrimack* or the *Monitor,* although there were black sailors in the Union Navy as early as 1861—as firemen, cooks, and stewards. At least one ship had a black gun crew, the U.S.S. *Minnesota,* a vessel the *Merrimack* fired on.

Our sources of background information are too varied to list separately. They range from the very many volumes of *Records of the Rebellion* to specialized books on the Confederate and Union ironclads. Norfolk Bay is familiar to one author inasmuch as he has often sailed its waters aboard his cutter, the *Chantey.*

For facts supplied us, we owe debts of gratitude to the reference staffs of the University of California, Riverside Library; to Peggy A. Haile of the Sargeant Memorial Room of the Norfolk Public Library, Norfolk, Virginia; the Command and General Staff College, Fort Leavenworth, Kansas; and to Benjamin H. Trask, reference librarian at the Mariners' Museum, Newport News, Virginia.

Patricia Beatty
Phillip Robbins
NOVEMBER 1989